Roald Dahl

Over to You

Ten stories of flyers and flying

Penguin Books

PENGUIN BOOKS

Published by the Penguin Group
Penguin Books Ltd, 27 Wrights Lane, London W8 5TZ, England
Penguin Putnam Inc., 375 Hudson Street, New York, New York 10014, USA
Penguin Books Australia Ltd, Ringwood, Victoria, Australia
Penguin Books Canada Ltd, 10 Alcorn Avenue, Toronto, Ontario, Canada M4V 3B2
Penguin Books (NZ) Ltd, Private Bag 102902, NSMC, Auckland, New Zealand

Penguin Books Ltd, Registered Offices: Harmondsworth, Middlesex, England

First published in the United States of America by Reynal & Hitchcock 1946
Published in Penguin Books 1973
31

Printed in England by Clays Ltd, St Ives plc
Set in Linotype Times

PENGUIN BOOKS

OVER TO YOU

Roald Dahl's parents were Norwegian, but he was born in Llandaff, Glamorgan, in 1916 and educated at Repton School. On the outbreak of the Second World War, he enlisted in the RAF at Nairobi. He was severely wounded after joining a fighter squadron in Libya, but later saw service as a fighter pilot in Greece and Syria. In 1942 he went to Washington as Assistant Air Attaché, which was where he started to write, and then was transferred to Intelligence, ending the war as a wing commander. His first twelve short stories, based on his wartime experiences, were originally published in leading American magazines and afterwards as a book, *Over to You*. All of his highly acclaimed stories have been widely translated and have become bestsellers all over the world. Anglia Television dramatized a selection of his short stories under the title *Tales of the Unexpected*. Among his other publications are two volumes of autobiography, *Boy* and *Going Solo*, his much-praised novel, *My Uncle Oswald*, and *Roald Dahl's Book of Ghost Stories*, of which he was editor. During the last year of his life he compiled a book of anecdotes and recipes with his wife, Felicity, which was published by Penguin in 1996 as *Roald Dahl's Cookbook*. One of the most successful and well known of all children's writers, his books are read by children all over the world. These include *James and the Giant Peach*, *Charlie and the Chocolate Factory*, *The Magic Finger*, *Charlie and the Great Glass Elevator*, *Fantastic Mr Fox*, *The Twits*, *The Witches*, winner of the 1983 Whitbread Award, *The BFG* and *Matilda*.

Roald Dahl died in November 1990. *The Times* described him as 'one of the most widely read and influential writers of our genera-tion' and wrote in its obituary: 'Children loved his stories and made him their favourite . . . They will be classics of the future.'

ROALD DAHL IN PENGUIN

Fiction
Over to You
Someone Like You
Kiss Kiss
Switch Bitch
Tales of the Unexpected
My Uncle Oswald
More Tales of the Unexpected
The Wonderful Story of Henry Sugar
The Best of Roald Dahl
Roald Dahl's Book of Ghost Stories (*editor*)
Completely Unexpected Tales
Ah, Sweet Mystery of Life
The Collected Short Stories of Roald Dahl

Non-Fiction
Boy
Going Solo
(*also published together in one volume*)
Roald Dahl's Cookbook
(*with Felicity Dahl*)

For S. M. D.

Contents

Acknowledgements

My sincere thanks to *The Saturday Evening Post*, *Tomorrow*, *Harper's Magazine*, *Ladies' Home Journal*, and *Town and Country*, in which some of these stories have previously been published.

I do not refer to anyone in particular in these stories. The names are not the names of pilots I have known; nor does the use of the personal pronoun necessarily mean that I am referring to myself.

Death of an Old Old Man

Oh God, how I am frightened.

Now that I am alone I don't have to hide it; I don't have to hide anything any longer. I can let my face go because no one can see me; because there's twenty-one thousand feet between me and them and because now that it's happening again I couldn't pretend any more even if I wanted to. Now I don't have to press my teeth together and tighten the muscles of my jaw as I did during lunch when the corporal brought in the message; when he handed it to Tinker and Tinker looked up at me and said, 'Charlie, it's your turn. You're next up.' As if I didn't know that. As if I didn't know that I was next up. As if I didn't know it last night when I went to bed, and at midnight when I was still awake and all the way through the night, at one in the morning and at two and three and four and five and six and at seven o'clock when I got up. As if I didn't know it while I was dressing and while I was having breakfast and while I was reading the magazines in the mess, playing shove-halfpenny in the mess, reading the notices in the mess, playing billiards in the mess. I knew it then and I knew it when we went in to lunch, while we were eating that mutton for lunch. And when the corporal came into the room with the message – it wasn't anything at all. It wasn't anything more than when it begins to rain because there is a black cloud in the sky. When he handed the paper to Tinker I knew what Tinker was going to say before he had opened his mouth. I knew exactly what he was going to say.

So that wasn't anything either.

But when he folded the message up and put it in his pocket and said, 'Finish your pudding. You've got plenty of time,' that was when it got worse, because I knew for certain then that it was going to happen again, that within half an hour I would be strapping myself in and testing the engine and signalling to the airmen to pull away the chocks. The others were all sitting around eating their pudding; mine was still on my plate in front of me, and I couldn't take another mouthful. But it was fine when I tightened my jaw muscles and said, 'Thank God for that. I'm tired of sitting around here picking my nose.' It was certainly fine when I said that. It must have sounded like any of the others just before they started off. And when I got up to leave the table and said, 'See you at tea time,' that must have sounded all right too.

But now I don't have to do any of that. Thank Christ I don't have to do that now. I can just loosen up and let myself go. I can do or say anything I want so long as I fly this aeroplane properly. It didn't use to be like this. Four years ago it was wonderful. I loved doing it because it was exciting, because the waiting on the aerodrome was nothing more than the waiting before a football game or before going in to bat; and three years ago it was all right too. But then always the three months of resting and the going back again and the resting and the going back; always going back and always getting away with it, everyone saying what a fine pilot, no one knowing what a near thing it was that time near Brussels and how lucky it was that time over Dieppe and how bad it was that other time over Dieppe and how lucky and bad and scared I've been every minute of every trip every week this year. No one knows that. They all say, 'Charlie's a great pilot,' 'Charlie's a born flyer,' 'Charlie's terrific.'

I think he was once, but not any longer.

Each time now it gets worse. At first it begins to grow upon you slowly, coming upon you slowly, creeping up on you from behind, making no noise, so that you do not turn round and see it coming. If you saw it coming, perhaps you could stop it, but there is no warning. It creeps closer and closer, like a cat creeps closer stalking a sparrow, and then when it is right behind you, it doesn't spring like the cat would spring; it just leans forward and whispers in your ear. It touches you gently on the shoulder and whispers to you that you are young, that you have a million things to do and a million things to say, that if you are not careful you will buy it, that you are almost certain to buy it sooner or later, and that when you do you will not be anything any longer; you will just be a charred corpse. It whispers to you about how your corpse will look when it is charred, how black it will be and how it will be twisted and brittle, with the face black and the fingers black and the shoes off the feet because the shoes always come off the feet when you die like that. At first it whispers to you only at night, when you are lying awake in bed at night. Then it whispers to you at odd moments during the day, when you are doing your teeth or drinking a beer or when you are walking down the passage; and in the end it becomes so that you hear it all day and all night all the time.

There's Ijmuiden. Just the same as ever, with the little knob sticking out just beside it. There are the Frisians, Texel, Vlieland, Terschelling, Ameland, Juist and Norderney. I know them all. They look like bacteria under a microscope. There's the Zuider Zee, there's Holland, there's the North Sea, there's Belgium, and there's the world; there's the whole bloody world right there, with all the people who aren't going to get killed and all the houses and the towns and the sea with all the fish. The fish aren't going to get killed either. I'm the only one that's going to get killed. I don't want to die. Oh God, I don't want to die. I don't want to die today anyway. And it isn't the pain. Really it isn't the pain. I don't mind having my leg mashed or my arm burnt off; I swear to you that I don't mind that. But I don't want to die. Four years ago I didn't mind. I remember distinctly not minding about it four years ago. I didn't mind about it three years ago either. It was all fine and exciting; it always is when it looks as though you may be going to lose, as it did then. It is always fine to fight when you are going to lose everything anyway, and that was how it was four years ago. But now we're going to win. It is so different when you are going to win. If I die now I lose fifty years of life, and I don't want to lose that. I'll lose anything except that because that would be all the things I want to do and all the things I want to see; all the things like going on

13

sleeping with Joey. Like going home sometimes. Like walking through a wood. Like pouring out a drink from a bottle. Like looking forward to week ends and like being alive every hour every day every year for fifty years. If I die now I will miss all that, and I will miss everything else. I will miss the things that I don't know about. I think those are really the things I am frightened of missing. I think the reason I do not want to die is because of the things I hope will happen. Yes, that's right. I'm sure that's right. Point a revolver at a tramp, at a wet shivering tramp on the side of the road and say, 'I'm going to shoot you,' and he will cry, 'Don't shoot. Please don't shoot.' The tramp clings to life because of the things he hopes will happen. I am clinging to it for the same reason; but I have clung for so long now that I cannot hold on much longer. Soon I will have to let go. It is like hanging over the edge of a cliff, that's what it is like; and I've been hanging on too long now, holding on to the top of the cliff with my fingers, not being able to pull myself back up, with my fingers getting more and more tired, beginning to hurt and to ache, so that I know that sooner or later I will have to let go. I dare not cry out for help; that is one thing that I dare not do; so I go on hanging over the side of this cliff, and as I hang I keep kicking a little with my feet against the side of the cliff, trying desperately to find a foothold, but it is steep and smooth like the side of a ship, and there isn't any foothold. I am kicking now, that's what I am doing. I am kicking against the smooth side of the cliff, and there isn't any foothold. Soon I shall have to let go. The longer I hang on the more certain I am of that, and so each hour, each day, each night, each week, I become more and more frightened. Four years ago I wasn't hanging over the edge like this. I was running about in the field above, and although I knew that there was a cliff somewhere and that I might fall over it, I did not mind. Three years ago it was the same, but now it is different.

I know that I am not a coward. I am certain of that. I will always keep going. Here I am today, at two o'clock in the afternoon, sitting here flying a course of one hundred and thirty-five at three hundred and sixty miles an hour and flying well; and although I am so frightened that I can hardly think, yet I am going on to do this thing. There was never any question of not going or of turning back. I would rather die than turn back. Turning back never enters into it. It would be easier if it did. I would prefer to have to fight that than to have to fight this fear.

There's Wassalt. Little camouflaged group of buildings and great big camouflaged aerodrome, probably full of one-o-nines and one-nineties. Holland looks wonderful. It must be a lovely place in the summer. I expect they are haymaking down there now. I expect the German soldiers are watching the Dutch girls haymaking. Bastards. Watching them haymaking, then making them come home with them afterwards. I would like to be haymaking now. I would like to be haymaking and drinking cider.

The pilot was sitting upright in the cockpit. His face was nearly hidden by his goggles and by his oxygen mask. His right hand was resting lightly upon the stick, and his left hand was forward on the throttle. All the time he was looking around him into the sky. From force of habit his head never ceased to move from one side to the other, slowly, mechanically, like clockwork, so that each moment almost, he searched every part of the blue sky, above, below and all around. But it was into the light of the sun itself that he looked twice as long as he looked anywhere else; for that is the place where the enemy hides and waits before he jumps upon you. There are only two places in which you can hide yourself when you are up in the sky. One is in cloud and the other is in the light of the sun.

He flew on; and although his mind was working upon many things and although his brain was the brain of a frightened man, yet his instinct was the instinct of a pilot who is in the sky of the enemy. With a quick glance, without stopping the movement of his head, he looked down and checked his instruments. The glance took no more than a second, and like a camera can record a dozen things at once with the opening of a shutter, so he at a glance recorded with his eyes his oil pressure, his petrol, his oxygen, his rev counter, boost and his air-speed, and in the same instant almost he was looking up again into the sky. He looked at the sun, and as he looked, as he screwed up his eyes and searched into the dazzling brightness of the sun, he thought that he saw something. Yes, there it was; a small black speck moving slowly across the bright surface of the sun, and to him the speck was not a speck but a life-size German pilot sitting in a Focke Wulf which had cannon in its wings.

He knew that he had been seen. He was certain that the one above was watching him, taking his time, sure of being hidden in the brightness of the sun, watching the Spitfire and waiting to pounce. The man in the Spitfire did not take his eye away from the small speck of black. His head was quite still now. He was watching the enemy, and as he watched, his left hand came away from the throttle and began to move delicately around the cockpit. It moved quickly and surely, touching this thing and that, switching on his reflector sight, turning his trigger button from 'safe' over to 'fire' and pressing gently with his thumb upon a lever which increased, ever so slightly, the pitch of the airscrew.

There was no thought in his head now save for the thought of battle. He was no longer frightened or thinking of being frightened. All that was a dream, and as a sleeper who opens his eyes in the morning and forgets his dream, so this man had seen the enemy and had forgotten that he was frightened. It was always the same. It had happened a hundred times before, and now it was happening again. Suddenly, in an instant he had become cool and precise, and as he prepared himself, as he made ready his cockpit, he watched the German, waiting to see what he would do.

This man was a great pilot. He was great because when the time came, whenever the moment arrived, his coolness was great and his courage was great, and more than anything else his instinct was great, greater by far than his coolness or his courage or his experience. Now he eased open the throttle and pulled the stick gently backwards, trying to gain height, trying to gain a little of the five-thousand-feet advantage which the German had over him. But there was not much time. The

Focke Wulf came out of the sun with its nose down and it came fast. The pilot saw it coming and he kept going straight on, pretending that he had not seen it, and all the time he was looking over his shoulder, watching the German, waiting for the moment to turn. If he turned too soon, the German would turn with him, and he would be duck soup. If he turned too late, the German would get him anyway provided that he could shoot straight, and he would be duck soup then too. So he watched and waited, turning his head and looking over his shoulder, judging his distance; and as the German came within range, as he was about to press his thumb upon the trigger button, the pilot swerved. He yanked the stick hard back and over to the left, he kicked hard with his left foot upon the rudder-bar, and like a leaf which is caught up and carried away by a gust of wind, the Spitfire flipped over on to its side and changed direction. The pilot blacked out.

As his sight came back, as the blood drained away from his head and from his eyes, he looked up and saw the German fighter 'way ahead, turning with him, banking hard, trying to turn tighter and tighter in order to get back on the tail of the Spitfire. The fight was on. 'Here we go,' he said to himself. 'Here we go again,' and he smiled once, quickly, because he was confident and because he had done this so many times before and because each time he had won.

The man was a beautiful pilot. But the German was good too, and when the Spitfire applied a little flap in order to turn in tighter circles, the Focke Wulf appeared to do the same, and they turned together. When the Spitfire throttled back suddenly and got on his tail, the Focke Wulf half-rolled and dived out and under and was away, pulling up again in a loop and rolling off the top, so that he came in again from behind. The Spitfire half-rolled and dived away, but the Focke Wulf anticipated him, and half-rolled and dived with him, behind him on his tail, and here he took a quick shot at the Spitfire, but he missed. For at least fifteen minutes the two small aircraft rolled and dived around each other in the sky. Sometimes they would separate, wheeling around and around in tight turns, watching one another, circling and watching like two boxers circling each other in the ring, waiting for an opening or for the dropping of a guard; then there would be a stall-turn and one would attack the other, and the diving and the rolling and the zooming would start all over again.

All the time the pilot of the Spitfire sat upright in his cockpit, and he flew his aircraft not with his hands but with the tips of his fingers, and the Spitfire was not a Spitfire but a part of his own body; the muscles of his arms and legs were in the wings and in the tail of the machine so that when he banked and turned and dived and climbed he was not moving his hands and his legs, but only the wings and the tail and the body of the aeroplane; for the body of the Spitfire was the body of the pilot, and there was no difference between the one and the other.

So it went on, and all the while, as they fought and as they flew, they lost height, coming down nearer and nearer to the fields of Holland, so that soon they were fighting only three thousand feet above the ground, and one could see the hedges and the small trees and shadows which the small trees made upon the grass.

Once the German tried a long shot, from a thousand yards, and the pilot of the Spitfire saw the tracer streaming past in front of the nose of his machine. Once, when they flew close past each other, he saw, for a moment, the head and shoulders of the German under the glass roof of his cockpit, the head turned towards him, with the brown helmet, the goggles, the nose and the white scarf. Once when he blacked out from a quick pull-out, the black-out lasted longer than usual. It lasted maybe five seconds, and when his sight came back, he looked quickly around for the Focke Wulf and saw it half a mile away, flying straight at him on the beam, a thin inch-long black line which grew quickly, so that almost at once it was no longer an inch, but an inch and a half, then two inches, then six and then a foot. There was hardly any time. There was a second or perhaps two at the most, but it was enough because he did not have to think or to wonder what to do; he had only to allow his instinct to control his arms and his legs and the wings and the body of the aeroplane. There was only one thing to do, and the Spitfire did it. It banked steeply and turned at right-angles towards the Focke Wulf, facing it and flying straight towards it for a head-on attack.

The two machines flew fast towards each other. The pilot of the Spitfire sat upright in his cockpit, and now, more than ever, the aircraft was a part of his body. His eye was upon the reflector sight, the small yellow electric-light dot which was projected up in front of the windshield, and it was upon the thinness of the Focke Wulf beyond. Quickly, precisely, he moved his aircraft a little this way and that, and the yellow dot, which moved with the aircraft, danced and jerked this way and that, and then suddenly it was upon the thin line of the Focke Wulf and there it stayed. His right thumb in the leather glove felt for the firing-button; he squeezed it gently, as a rifleman squeezes a trigger, his guns fired, and at the same time, he saw the small spurts of flame from the cannon in the nose of the Focke Wulf. The whole thing, from beginning to end, took perhaps as long as it would take you to light a cigarette. The German pilot came straight on at him and he had a sudden, vivid, colourless view of the round nose and the thin outstretched wings of the Focke Wulf. Then there was a crack as their wing-tips met, and there was a splintering as the port wing of the Spitfire came away from the body of the machine.

The Spitfire was dead. It fell like a dead bird falls, fluttering a little as it died; continuing in the direction of its flight as it fell. The hands of the pilot, almost in a single movement, undid his straps, tore off his helmet and slid back the hood of the cockpit; then they grasped the edges of the cockpit and he was out and away, falling, reaching for the ripcord, grasping it with his right hand, pulling on it so that his parachute billowed out and opened and the straps jerked him hard between the fork of his legs.

All of a sudden the silence was great. The wind was blowing on his face and in his hair and he reached up a hand and brushed the hair away from his eyes. He was about a thousand feet up, and he looked down and saw flat green country with fields and hedges and no trees. He could see some cows in the

field below him. Then he looked up, and as he looked, he said
'Good God,' and his right hand moved quickly to his right hip,
feeling for his revolver which he had not brought with him.
For there, not more than five hundred yards away, parachut-
ing down at the same time and at the same height, was another
man, and he knew when he saw him that it could be only the
German pilot. Obviously his plane had been damaged at the
same time as the Spitfire in the collision. He must have got out
quickly too; and now here they were, both of them parachut-
ing down so close to each other that they might even land in
the same field.

He looked again at the German, hanging there in his straps
with his legs apart, his hands above his head grasping the cords
of the parachute. He seemed to be a small man, thickly built
and by no means young. The German was looking at him too.
He kept looking, and when his body swung around the other
way, he turned his head, looking over his shoulder.

So they went on down. Both men were watching each other,
thinking about what would happen soon, and the German was
the king because he was landing in his own territory. The pilot
of the Spitfire was coming down in enemy country; he would
be taken prisoner, or he would be killed, or he would kill the
German, and if he did that, he would escape. I will escape
anyway, he thought. I'm sure I can run faster than the German. He does not look as though he could run very fast. I will
race him across the fields and get away.

The ground was close now. There were not many seconds to
go. He saw that the German would almost certainly land in
the same field as he, the field with the cows. He looked down
to see what the field was like and whether the hedges were
thick and whether there was a gate in the hedge, and as he
looked, he saw below him in the field a small pond, and there
was a small stream running through the pond. It was a cow-
drinking pond, muddy round the edges and muddy in the
water. The pond was right below him. He was no more than
the height of a horse above it and he was dropping fast;
he was dropping right into the middle of the pond. Quickly he
grasped the cords above his head and tried to spill the para-

chute to one side so that he would change direction, but he was too late; it wasn't any good. All at once something brushed the surface of his brain and the top of his stomach, and the fear which he had forgotten in the fighting was upon him again. He saw the pond and the black surface of the water of the pond, and the pond was not a pond, and the water was not water; it was a small black hole in the surface of the earth which went on down and down for miles and miles, with steep smooth sides like the sides of a ship, and it was so deep that when you fell into it, you went on falling and falling and you fell for ever. He saw the mouth of the hole and the deepness of it, and he was only a small brown pebble which someone had picked up and thrown into the air so that it would fall into the hole. He was a pebble which someone had picked up in the grass of the field. That was all he was and now he was falling and the hole was below him.

Splash. He hit the water. He went through the water and his feet hit the bottom of the pond. They sank into the mud on the bottom and his head went under the water, but it came up again and he was standing with the water up to his shoulders. The parachute was on top of him; his head was tangled in a mass of cords and white silk and he pulled at them with his hands, first this way and then that, but it only got worse, and the fear got worse because the white silk was covering his head so that he could see nothing but a mass of white cloth and a tangle of cords. Then he tried to move towards the bank, but his feet were stuck in the mud; he had sunk up to his knees in the mud. So he fought the parachute and the tangled cords of the parachute, pulling at them with his hands and trying to get them clear of his head; and as he did so he heard the sound of footsteps running on the grass. He heard the noise of the footsteps coming closer and the German must have jumped, because there was a splash and he was knocked over by the weight of a man's body.

He was under the water, and instinctively he began to struggle. But his feet were still stuck in the mud, the man was on top of him and there were hands around his neck holding him under and squeezing his neck with strong fingers. He opened his eyes and saw brown water. He noticed the bubbles in the water, small bright bubbles rising slowly upward in the brown water. There was no noise or shouting or anything else, but only the bright bubbles moving upward in the water, and suddenly, as he watched them, his mind became clear and calm like a sunny day. I won't struggle, he thought. There is no point in struggling, for when there is a black cloud in the sky, it is bound to rain.

He relaxed his body and all the muscles in his body because he had no further wish to struggle. How nice it is not to struggle, he thought. There is no point in struggling. I was a fool to have struggled so much and for so long; I was a fool to have prayed for the sun when there was a black cloud in the sky. I should have prayed for rain; I should have shouted for rain. I should have shouted, Let it rain, let it rain in solid sheets and I will not care. Then it would have been easy. It would have been so easy then. I have struggled for five years and now I don't have to do it any more. This is so much better; this is ever so much better, because there is a wood somewhere that I wish to walk through, and you cannot walk struggling through a wood. There is a girl somewhere that I wish to sleep with, and you cannot sleep struggling with a girl. You cannot do anything struggling; especially you cannot live struggling, and so now I am going to do all the things that I want to do, and there will be no more struggling.

See how calm and lovely it is like this. See how sunny it is and what a beautiful field this is, with the cows and the little pond and the green hedges with primroses growing in the hedges. Nothing will worry me any more now, nothing nothing nothing; not even that man splashing in the water of the pond over there. He seems very puffed and out of breath. He seems to be dragging something out of the pond, something heavy. Now he's got it to the side and he's pulling it up on to the grass. How funny; it's a body. It's a body of a man. As a matter of fact, I think it's me. Yes, it is me. I know it is because of that smudge of yellow paint on the front of my flying suit. Now he's kneeling down, searching in my pockets, taking out my money and my identification card. He's found my pipe and the letter I got this morning from my mother. He's taking off my watch. Now he's getting up. He's going away. He's going to leave my body behind, lying on the grass beside the pond. He's walking quickly away across the field towards the gate. How wet and excited he looks. He ought to relax a bit. He ought to relax like me. He can't be enjoying himself that way. I think I will tell him.

'Why don't you relax a bit?'

Goodness, how he jumped when I spoke to him. And his face; just look at his face. I've never seen a man look as frightened as that. He's starting to run. He keeps looking back over his shoulder, but he keeps on running. But just look at his face; just look how unhappy and frightened he is. I do not want to go with him. I think I'll leave him. I think I'll stay here for a bit. I think I'll go along the hedges and find some primroses, and if I am lucky I may find some white violets. Then I will go to sleep. I will go to sleep in the sun.

An African Story

For England, the war began in September, 1939. The people on the island knew about it at once and began to prepare themselves. In farther places the people heard about it a few minutes afterwards, and they too began to prepare themselves.

And in East Africa, in Kenya Colony, there was a young man who was a white hunter, who loved the plains and the valleys and the cool nights on the slopes of Kilimanjaro. He too heard about the war and began to prepare himself. He made his way over the country to Nairobi, and he reported to the R.A.F. and asked that they make him a pilot. They took him in and he began his training at Nairobi airport, flying in little Tiger Moths and doing well with his flying.

After five weeks he nearly got court-martialled because he took his plane up and instead of practising spins and stall-turns as he had been ordered to do, he flew off in the direction of Nakuru to look at the wild animals on the plain. On the way, he thought he saw a Sable antelope, and because these are rare animals, he became excited and flew down low to get a better view. He was looking down at the antelope out of the left side of the cockpit, and because of this he did not see the giraffe on the other side. The leading edge of the starboard wing struck the neck of the giraffe just below the head and cut clean through it. He was flying as low as that. There was damage to the wing, but he managed to get back to Nairobi, and as I said, he was nearly court-martialled, because you cannot explain away a thing like that by saying you hit a large bird, not when there are pieces of giraffe skin and giraffe hair sticking to the wing and the stays.

After six weeks he was allowed to make his first solo cross-country flight, and he flew off from Nairobi to a place called Eldoret, which is a little town eight thousand feet up in the Highlands. But again he was unlucky. This time he had engine failure on the way, due to water in the fuel tanks. He kept his head and made a beautiful forced landing without damaging the aircraft, not far from a little shack which stood alone on the highland plain with no other habitation in sight. That is lonely country up there.

He walked over to the shack, and there he found an old man, living alone, with nothing but a small patch of sweet potatoes, some brown chickens and a black cow.

The old man was kind to him. He gave him food and milk and a place to sleep, and the pilot stayed with him for two days and two nights, until a rescue plane from Nairobi spotted his aircraft on the ground, landed beside it, found out what was wrong, went away and came back with clean petrol which enabled him to take off and return.

But during his stay, the old man, who was lonely and had seen no one for many months, was glad of his company and of the opportunity to talk. He talked much and the pilot listened. He talked of the lonely life, of the lions that came in the night, of the rogue elephant that lived over the hill in the west, of the hotness of the days and of the silence that came with the cold at midnight.

On the second night he talked about himself. He told a long, strange story, and as he told it, it seemed to the pilot that the old man was lifting a great weight off his shoulders in the telling. When he had finished, he said that he had never told that to anyone before, and that he would never tell it to anyone again, but the story was so strange that the pilot wrote it down on paper as soon as he got back to Nairobi. He wrote it not in the old man's words, but in his own words, painting it as a picture with the old man as a character in the picture, because that was the best way to do it. He had never written a story before, and so naturally there were mistakes. He did not know any of the tricks with words which writers use, which they have to use just as painters have to use tricks with paint, but when he had finished writing, when he put down his pencil and went over to the airmen's canteen for a pint of beer, he left behind him a rare and powerful tale.

We found it in his suitcase two weeks later when we were going through his belongings after he had been killed in training, and because he seemed to have no relatives, and because he was my friend, I took the manuscript and looked after it for him.

This is what he wrote.

*

The old man came out of the door into the bright sunshine, and for a moment he stood leaning on his stick, looking around him, blinking at the strong light. He stood with his head on one side, looking up, listening for the noise which he thought he had heard.

He was small and thick and well over seventy years old, although he looked nearer eighty-five, because rheumatism had tied his body into knots. His face was covered with grey hair, and when he moved his mouth, he moved it only on one side of his face. On his head, whether indoors or out, he wore a dirty white topee.

He stood quite still in the bright sunshine, screwing up his eyes, listening for the noise.

Yes, there it was again. The head of the old man flicked around and he looked towards the small wooden hut standing a hundred yards away on the pasture. This time there was no doubt about it: the yelp of a dog, the high-pitched, sharp-piercing yelp of pain which a dog gives when he is in great danger. Twice more it came and this time the noise was more like a scream than a yelp. The note was higher and more sharp, as though it were wrenched quickly from some small place inside the body.

The old man turned and limped fast across the grass towards the wooden shed where Judson lived, pushed open the door and went in.

The small white dog was lying on the floor and Judson was standing over it, his legs apart, his black hair falling all over his long, red face; standing there tall and skinny, muttering to himself and sweating through his greasy white shirt. His mouth hung open in an odd way, lifeless way, as though his jaw was too heavy for him, and he was dribbling gently down the middle of his chin. He stood there looking at the small white dog which was lying on the floor, and with one hand he was slowly twisting his left ear; in the other he held a heavy bamboo.

The old man ignored Judson and went down on his knees beside his dog, gently running his thin hands over its body. The dog lay still, looking up at him with watery eyes. Judson did not move. He was watching the dog and the man.

Slowly the old man got up, rising with difficulty, holding the top of his stick with both hands and pulling himself to his feet. He looked around the room. There was a dirty rumpled mattress lying on the floor in the far corner; there was a wooden table made of packing cases and on it a Primus stove and a chipped blue-enamelled saucepan. There were chicken feathers and mud on the floor.

The old man saw what he wanted. It was a heavy iron bar standing against the wall near the mattress, and he hobbled over towards it, thumping the hollow wooden floorboards with his stick as he went. The eyes of the dog followed his movements as he limped across the room. The old man changed his stick to his left hand, took the iron bar in his right, hobbled back to the dog and without pausing, he lifted the bar and brought it down hard upon the animal's head. He threw the bar to the ground and looked up at Judson, who was standing there with his legs apart, dribbling down his chin and twitching around the corners of his eyes. He went right up to him and began to speak. He spoke very quietly and slowly, with a terrible anger, and as he spoke he moved only one side of his mouth.

'You killed him,' he said. 'You broke his back.'

Then, as the tide of anger rose and gave him strength, he found more words. He looked up and spat them into the face of the tall Judson, who twitched around the corners of his eyes and backed away towards the wall.

'You lousy, mean, dog-beating bastard. That was my dog.

27

What the hell right have you got beating my dog, tell me that. Answer me, you slobbering madman. Answer me.'

Judson was slowly rubbing the palm of his left hand up and down on the front of his shirt, and now the whole of his face began to twitch. Without looking up, he said, 'He wouldn't stop licking that old place on his paw. I couldn't stand the noise it made. You know I can't stand noises like that, licking, licking, licking. I told him to stop. He looked up and wagged his tail; but then he went on licking. I couldn't stand it any longer, so I beat him.'

The old man did not say anything. For a moment it looked as though he were going to hit this creature. He half raised his arm, dropped it again, spat on the floor, turned around and hobbled out of the door into the sunshine. He went across the grass to where a black cow was standing in the shade of a small acacia tree, chewing its cud, and the cow watched him as he came limping across the grass from the shed. But it went on chewing, munching its cud, moving its jaws regularly, mechanically, like a metronome in slow time. The old man came limping up and stood beside it, stroking its neck. Then he leant against its shoulder and scratched its back with the butt-end of his stick. He stood there for a long time, leaning against the cow, scratching it with his stick; and now and again he would speak to it, speaking quiet little words, whispering them almost, like a person telling a secret to another.

It was shady under the acacia tree, and the country around him looked lush and pleasant after the long rains, for the grass grows green up in the Highlands of Kenya; and at this time of the year, after the rains, it is as green and rich as any grass in the world. Away in the north stood Mount Kenya itself, with snow upon its head, with a thin white plume trailing from its summit where the icy winds made a storm and blew the white powder from the top of the mountain. Down below, upon the slopes of that same mountain there were lion and elephant, and sometimes during the night one could hear the roar of the lions as they looked at the moon.

The days passed and Judson went about his work on the farm in a silent, mechanical kind of way, taking in the corn,

digging the sweet potatoes and milking the black cow, while
the old man stayed indoors away from the fierce African sun.
Only in the late afternoon when the air began to get cool and
sharp, did he hobble outside, and always he went over to his
black cow and spent an hour with it under the acacia tree. One
day when he came out he found Judson standing beside the
cow, regarding it strangely, standing in a peculiar attitude with
one foot in front of the other and gently twisting his ear with
his right hand.

'What is it now?' said the old man as he came limping up.

'Cow won't stop chewing,' said Judson.

'Chewing her cud,' said the old man. 'Leave her alone.'

Judson said, 'It's the noise, can't you hear it? Crunchy noise
like she was chewing pebbles, only she isn't; she's chewing
grass and spit. Look at her, she goes on and on crunching,
crunching, crunching, and it's just grass and spit. Noise goes
right into my head.'

'Get out,' said the old man. 'Get out of my sight.'

At dawn the old man sat, as he always did, looking out of
his window, watching Judson coming across from his hut to
milk the cow. He saw him coming sleepily across the field,
talking to himself as he walked, dragging his feet, making
a dark green trail in the wet grass, carrying in his hand the old
four-gallon kerosene tin which he used as a milk pail. The sun
was coming up over the escarpment and making long shadows
behind the man, the cow and the little acacia tree. The old man
saw Judson put down the tin and he saw him fetch the box
from beside the acacia tree and settle himself upon it, ready
for the milking. He saw him suddenly kneeling down, feeling
the udder of the cow with his hands and at the same time the
old man noticed from where he sat that the animal had no
milk. He saw Judson get up and come walking fast towards the
shack. He came and stood under the window where the old
man was sitting and looked up.

'Cow's got no milk,' he said.

The old man leaned through the open window, placing both
his hands on the sill.

'You lousy bastard, you've stole it.'

'I didn't take it,' said Judson. 'I bin asleep.'

'You stole it.' The old man was leaning farther out of the window, speaking quietly with one side of his mouth. 'I'll beat the hell out of you for this,' he said.

Judson said, 'Someone stole it in the night, a native, one of the Kikuyu. Or maybe she's sick.'

It seemed to the old man that he was telling the truth. 'We'll see,' he said, 'if she milks this evening; and now for Christ's sake, get out of my sight.'

By evening the cow had a full udder and the old man watched Judson draw two quarts of good thick milk from under her.

The next morning she was empty. In the evening she was full. On the third morning she was empty once more.

On the third night the old man went on watch. As soon as it began to get dark, he stationed himself at the open window with an old twelve-bore shot gun lying on his lap, waiting for the thief who came and milked his cow in the night. At first it was pitch dark and he could not see the cow even, but soon a three-quarter moon came over the hills and it became light, almost as though it was day time. But it was bitter cold because the Highlands are seven thousand feet up, and the old man shivered at his post and pulled his brown blanket closer around his shoulders. He could see the cow well now, just as well as in daylight, and the little acacia tree threw a deep shadow across the grass, for the moon was behind it.

All through the night the old man sat there watching the cow, and save when he got up once and hobbled back into the room to fetch another blanket, his eyes never left her. The cow stood placidly under the small tree, chewing her cud and gazing at the moon.

An hour before dawn her udder was full. The old man could see it; he had been watching it the whole time, and although he had not seen the movement of its swelling any more than one can see the movement of the hour hand of a watch, yet all the time he had been conscious of the filling as the milk came down. It was an hour before dawn. The moon was low, but the light had not gone. He could see the cow and the little tree and the greenness of the grass around the cow. Suddenly he jerked his head. He heard something. Surely that was a noise he heard. Yes, there it was again, a rustling in the grass right underneath the window where he was sitting. Quickly he pulled himself up and looked over the sill on to the ground.

Then he saw it. A large black snake, a Mamba, eight feet long and as thick as a man's arm, was gliding through the wet grass, heading straight for the cow and going fast. Its small pear-shaped head was raised slightly off the ground and the movement of its body against the wetness made a clear hissing sound like gas escaping from a jet. He raised his gun to shoot. Almost at once he lowered it again, why he did not know, and he sat there not moving, watching the Mamba as it approached the cow, listening to the noise it made as it went, watching it come up close to the cow and waiting for it to strike.

But it did not strike. It lifted its head and for a moment let it sway gently back and forth; then it raised the front part of its black body into the air under the udder of the cow, gently took one of the thick teats into its mouth and began to drink.

The cow did not move. There was no noise anywhere, and the body of the Mamba curved gracefully up from the ground and hung under the udder of the cow. Black snake and black cow were clearly visible out there in the moonlight.

For half an hour the old man watched the Mamba taking the milk of the cow. He saw the gentle pulsing of its black body as it drew the liquid out of the udder and he saw it, after a time, change from one teat to another, until at last there was no longer any milk left. Then the Mamba gently lowered itself to the ground and slid back through the grass in the direction whence it came. Once more it made a clear hissing noise as it went, and once more it passed underneath the window where the old man sat, leaving a thin dark trail in the wet grass where it had gone. Then it disappeared behind the shack.

Slowly the moon went down behind the ridge of Mount Kenya. Almost at the same time the sun rose up out of the escarpment in the east and Judson came out of his hut with the four-gallon kerosene tin in his hand, walking sleepily towards the cow, dragging his feet in the heavy dew as he went. The old man watched him coming and waited. Judson bent down and felt the udder with his hand and as he did so, the old man shouted at him. Judson jumped at the sound of the old man's voice.

'It's gone again,' said the old man.

Judson said, 'Yes, cow's empty.'

'I think,' said the old man slowly, 'I think that it was a Kikuyu boy. I was dozing a bit and only woke up as he was making off. I couldn't shoot because the cow was in the way. He made off behind the cow. I'll wait for him tonight. I'll get him tonight,' he added.

Judson did not answer. He picked up his four-gallon tin and walked back to his hut.

That night the old man sat up again by the window watching the cow. For him there was this time a certain pleasure in the anticipation of what he was going to see. He knew that he would see the Mamba again, but he wanted to make quite certain. And so, when the great black snake slid across the grass towards the cow an hour before sunrise, the old man leaned over the window sill and followed the movements of the Mamba as it approached the cow. He saw it wait for a moment under the belly of the animal, letting its head sway slowly backwards and forwards half a dozen times before finally raising its body from the ground to take the teat of the cow into its mouth. He saw it drink the milk for half an hour, until there was none left, and he saw it lower its body and slide smoothly back behind the shack whence it came. And while he watched these things, the old man began laughing quietly with one side of his mouth.

Then the sun rose up from behind the hills, and Judson came out of his hut with the four-gallon tin in his hand, but this time he went straight to the window of the shack where the old man was sitting wrapped up in his blankets.

'What happened?' said Judson.

The old man looked down at him from his window. 'Nothing,' he said. 'Nothing happened. I dozed off again and the bastard came and took it while I was asleep. Listen, Judson,' he added, 'we got to catch this boy, otherwise you'll be going short of milk, not that that would do you any harm. But we got to catch him. I can't shoot because he's too clever; the cow's always in the way. You'll have to get him.'

'Me get him? How?'

The old man spoke very slowly. 'I think,' he said, 'I think you must hide beside the cow, right beside the cow. That is the only way you can catch him.'

Judson was rumpling his hair with his left hand.

'Today,' continued the old man, 'you will dig a shallow trench right beside the cow. If you lie in it and if I cover you over with hay and grass, the thief won't notice you until he's right alongside.'

'He may have a knife,' Judson said.

'No, he won't have a knife. You take your stick. That's all you'll need.'

Judson said, 'Yes, I'll take my stick. When he comes, I'll jump up and beat him with my stick.' Then suddenly he seemed to remember something. 'What about her chewing?' he said. 'Couldn't stand her chewing all night, crunching and crunching, crunching spit and grass like it was pebbles. Couldn't stand that all night,' and he began twisting again at his left ear with his hand.

'You'll do as you're bloody well told,' said the old man.

That day Judson dug his trench beside the cow which was to be tethered to the small acacia tree so that she could not wander about the field. Then, as evening came and as he was preparing to lie down in the trench for the night, the old man came to the door of his shack and said, 'No point in doing anything until early morning. They won't come till the cow's full. Come in here and wait; it's warmer than your filthy little hut.'

Judson had never been invited into the old man's shack before. He followed him in, happy that he would not have to lie all night in the trench. There was a candle burning in the room. It was stuck into the neck of a beer bottle and the bottle was on the table.

'Make some tea,' said the old man, pointing to the Primus

stove standing on the floor. Judson lit the stove and made tea. The two of them sat down on a couple of wooden boxes and began to drink. The old man drank his hot and made loud sucking noises as he drank. Judson kept blowing on his, sipping it cautiously and watching the old man over the top of his cup. The old man went on sucking away at his tea until suddenly Judson said, 'Stop.' He said it quietly, plaintively almost, and as he said it he began to twitch around the corners of his eyes and around his mouth.

'What?' said the old man.

Judson said, 'That noise, that sucking noise you're making.'

The old man put down his cup and regarded the other quietly for a few moments, then he said, 'How many dogs you killed in your time, Judson?'

There was no answer.

'I said how many? How many dogs?'

Judson began picking the tea leaves out of his cup and sticking them on to the back of his left hand. The old man was leaning forward on his box.

'How many dogs, Judson?'

Judson began to hurry with his tea leaves. He jabbed his fingers into his empty cup, picked out a tea leaf, pressed it quickly on to the back of his hand and quickly went back for another. When there were not many left and he did not find one immediately, he bent over and peered closely into the cup, trying to find the ones that remained. The back of the hand which held the cup was covered with wet black tea leaves.

'Judson!' The old man shouted, and one side of his mouth opened and shut like a pair of tongs. The candle flame flickered and became still again.

Then quietly and very slowly, coaxingly, as someone to a child. 'In all your life, how many dogs has it been?'

Judson said, 'Why should I tell you?' He did not look up. He was picking the tea leaves off the back of his hand one by one and returning them to the cup.

'I want to know, Judson.' The old man was speaking very gently. 'I'm getting keen about this too. Let's talk about it and make some plans for more fun.'

Judson looked up. A ball of saliva rolled down his chin, hung for a moment in the air, snapped and fell to the floor.

'I only kill 'em because of a noise.'

'How often've you done it? I'd love to know how often.'

'Lots of times long ago.'

'How? Tell me how you used to do it. What way did you like best?'

No answer.

'Tell me, Judson. I'd love to know.'

'I don't see why I should. It's a secret.'

'I won't tell. I swear I won't tell.'

'Well, if you'll promise.' Judson shifted his seat closer and spoke in a whisper. 'Once I waited till one was sleeping, then I got a big stone and dropped it on his head.'

The old man got up and poured himself a cup of tea. 'You didn't kill mine like that.'

'I didn't have time. The noise was so bad, the licking, and I just had to do it quick.'

'You didn't even kill him.'

'I stopped the noise.'

The old man went over to the door and looked out. It was dark. The moon had not yet risen, but the night was clear and cold with many stars. In the east there was a little paleness in the sky, and as he watched, the paleness grew and it changed from a paleness into a brightness, spreading over the sky so that the light was reflected and held by the small drops of dew upon the grass along the highlands; and slowly, the moon rose up over the hills. The old man turned and said, 'Better get ready. Never know; they might come early tonight.'

Judson got up and the two of them went outside. Judson lay down in the shallow trench beside the cow and the old man covered him over with grass, so that only his head peeped out above the ground. 'I shall be watching, too,' he said, 'from the window. If I give a shout, jump up and catch him.'

He hobbled back to the shack, went upstairs, wrapped himself in blankets and took up his position by the window. It was early still. The moon was nearly full and it was climbing. It shone upon the snow on the summit of Mount Kenya.

After an hour the old man shouted out of the window:

'Are you still awake, Judson?'

'Yes,' he answered, 'I'm awake.'

'Don't go to sleep,' said the old man. 'Whatever you do, don't go to sleep.'

'Cow's crunching all the time,' said Judson.

'Good, and I'll shoot you if you get up now,' said the old man.

'You'll shoot me?'

'I said I'll shoot you if you get up now.'

A gentle sobbing noise came up from where Judson lay, a strange gasping sound as though a child was trying not to cry, and in the middle of it, Judson's voice, 'I've got to move; please let me move. This crunching.'

'If you get up,' said the old man, 'I'll shoot you in the belly.'

For another hour or so the sobbing continued, then quite suddenly it stopped.

Just before four o'clock it began to get very cold and the old man huddled deeper into his blankets and shouted, 'Are you cold out there, Judson? Are you cold?'

'Yes,' came the answer. 'So cold. But I don't mind because cow's not crunching any more. She's asleep.'

The old man said, 'What are you going to do with the thief when you catch him?'

'I don't know.'

'Will you kill him?'

A pause.

'I don't know. I'll just go for him.'

'I'll watch,' said the old man. 'It ought to be fun.' He was leaning out of the window with his arms resting on the sill.

Then he heard the hiss under the window sill, and looked over and saw the black Mamba, sliding through the grass towards the cow, going fast and holding its head just a little above the ground as it went.

When the Mamba was five yards away, the old man shouted. He cupped his hands to his mouth and shouted, 'Here he comes, Judson; here he comes. Go and get him.'

Judson lifted his head quickly and looked up. As he did so

he saw the Mamba and the Mamba saw him. There was a second, or perhaps two, when the snake stopped, drew back and raised the front part of its body in the air. Then the stroke. Just a flash of black and a slight thump as it took him in the chest. Judson screamed, a long, high-pitched scream which did not rise nor fall, but held its note until gradually it faded into nothingness and there was silence. Now he was standing up, ripping open his shirt, feeling for the place in his chest, whimpering quietly, moaning and breathing hard with his mouth wide open. And all the while the old man sat quietly at the open window, leaning forward and never taking his eyes away from the one below.

Everything comes very quick when one is bitten by a black Mamba, and almost at once the poison began to work. It threw him to the ground, where he lay humping his back and rolling around on the grass. He no longer made any noise. It was all very quiet, as though a man of great strength was wrestling with a giant whom one could not see, and it was as though the giant was twisting him and not letting him get up, stretching his arms through the fork of his legs and pushing his knees up under his chin.

Then he began pulling up the grass with his hands and soon after that he lay on his back kicking gently with his legs. But he didn't last very long. He gave a quick wriggle, humped his back again, turning over as he did it, then he lay on the ground quite still, lying on his stomach with his right knee drawn up underneath his chest and his hands stretched out above his head.

Still the old man sat by the window, and even after it was all over, he stayed where he was and did not stir. There was a movement in the shadow under the acacia tree and the Mamba came forward slowly towards the cow. It came forward a little, stopped, raised its head, waited, lowered its head, and slid forward again right under the belly of the animal. It raised itself into the air and took one of the brown teats in its mouth and began to drink. The old man sat watching the Mamba taking the milk of the cow, and once again he saw the gentle pulsing of its body as it drew the liquid out of the udder.

While the snake was still drinking, the old man got up and moved away from the window.

'You can have his share,' he said quietly. 'We don't mind you having his share,' and as he spoke he glanced back and saw again the black body of the Mamba curving upward from the ground, joining with the belly of the cow.

'Yes,' he said again, 'we don't mind your having his share.'

A Piece of Cake

I do not remember much of it; not beforehand anyway; not until it happened.

There was the landing at Fouka, where the Blenheim boys were helpful and gave us tea while we were being refuelled. I remember the quietness of the Blenheim boys, how they came into the mess-tent to get some tea and sat down to drink it without saying anything; how they got up and went out when they had finished drinking and still they did not say anything. And I knew that each one was holding himself together because the going was not very good right then. They were having to go out too often, and there were no replacements coming along.

We thanked them for the tea and went out to see if they had finished refuelling our Gladiators. I remember that there was a wind blowing which made the windsock stand out straight, like a signpost, and the sand was blowing up around our legs and making a rustling noise as it swished against the tents, and the tents flapped in the wind so that they were like canvas men clapping their hands.

'Bomber boys unhappy,' Peter said.

'Not unhappy,' I answered.

'Well, they're browned off.'

'No. They've had it, that's all. But they'll keep going. You can see they're trying to keep going.'

Our two old Gladiators were standing beside each other in the sand and the airmen in their khaki shirts and shorts seemed still to be busy with the refuelling. I was wearing a thin white cotton flying suit and Peter had on a blue one. It wasn't necessary to fly with anything warmer.

Peter said, 'How far away is it?'

'Twenty-one miles beyond Charing Cross,' I answered, 'on

the right side of the road.' Charing Cross was where the desert road branched north to Mersah Matruh. The Italian army was outside Mersah, and they were doing pretty well. It was about the only time, so far as I know, that the Italians have done pretty well. Their morale goes up and down like a sensitive altimeter, and right then it was at forty thousand because the Axis was on top of the world. We hung around waiting for the refuelling to finish.

Peter said, 'It's a piece of cake.'

'Yes. It ought to be easy.'

We separated and I climbed into my cockpit. I have always remembered the face of the airman who helped me to strap in. He was oldish, about forty, and bald except for a neat patch of golden hair at the back of his head. His face was all wrinkles, his eyes were like my grandmother's eyes, and he looked as though he had spent his life helping to strap in pilots who never came back. He stood on the wing pulling my straps and said, 'Be careful. There isn't any sense not being careful.'

'Piece of cake,' I said.

'Like hell.'

'Really. It isn't anything at all. It's a piece of cake.'

I don't remember much about the next bit; I only remember about later on. I suppose we took off from Fouka and flew west towards Mersah, and I suppose we flew at about eight hundred feet. I suppose we saw the sea to starboard, and I suppose – no, I am certain – that it was blue and that it was beautiful, especially where it rolled up on to the sand and made a long thick white line east and west as far as you could see. I suppose we flew over Charing Cross and flew on for twenty-one miles to where they had said it would be, but I do not know. I know only that there was trouble, lots and lots of trouble, and I know that we had turned round and were coming back when the trouble got worse. The biggest trouble of all was that I was too low to bale out, and it is from that point on that my memory comes back to me. I remember the dipping of the nose of the aircraft and I remember looking down the nose of the machine at the ground and seeing a little clump of camel-thorn growing there all by itself. I remember seeing some rocks lying in the sand beside the camel-thorn, and the camel-thorn and the sand and the rocks leapt out of the ground and came to me. I remember that very clearly.

Then there was a small gap of not-remembering. It might have been one second or it might have been thirty; I do not know. I have an idea that it was very short, a second perhaps, and next I heard a *crumph* on the right as the starboard wing tank caught fire, then another *crumph* on the left as the port tank did the same. To me that was not significant, and for a while I sat still, feeling comfortable, but a little drowsy. I couldn't see with my eyes, but that was not significant either. There was nothing to worry about. Nothing at all. Not until I felt the hotness around my legs. At first it was only a warmness and that was all right too, but all at once it was a hotness, a very stinging scorching hotness up and down the sides of each leg.

I knew that the hotness was unpleasant, but that was all I knew. I disliked it, so I curled my legs up under the seat and waited. I think there was something wrong with the telegraph system between the body and the brain. It did not seem to be working very well. Somehow it was a bit slow in telling the brain all about it and in asking for instructions. But I believe a message eventually got through, saying, 'Down here there is a great hotness. What shall we do? (Signed) Left Leg and Right Leg.' For a long time there was no reply. The brain was figuring the matter out.

Then slowly, word by word, the answer was tapped over the wires. 'The – plane – is – burning. Get – out – repeat – get – out – get – out.' The order was relayed to the whole system, to all the muscles in the legs, arms and body, and the muscles went to work. They tried their best; they pushed a little and pulled a little, and they strained greatly, but it wasn't any good. Up went another telegram, 'Can't get out. Something holding us in.' The answer to this one took even longer in arriving, so I just sat there waiting for it to come, and all the time the hotness increased. Something was holding me down and it was up to the brain to find out what it was. Was it giants' hands pressing on my shoulders, or heavy stones or houses or steam rollers or filing cabinets or gravity or was it ropes? Wait a minute. Ropes – ropes. The message was beginning to come through. It came very slowly. 'Your – straps. Undo – your – straps.' My arms received the message and went to work. They tugged at the straps, but they wouldn't undo. They tugged again and again, a little feebly, but as hard as they could, and it wasn't any use. Back went the message, 'How do we undo the straps?'

This time I think that I sat there for three or four minutes waiting for the answer. It wasn't any use hurrying or getting impatient. That was the one thing of which I was sure. But what a long time it was all taking. I said aloud, 'Bugger it. I'm going to be burnt. I'm ...' but I was interrupted. The answer was coming – no, it wasn't – yes, it was, it was slowly coming through. 'Pull – out – the – quick – release – pin – you – bloody – fool – and – hurry.'

Out came the pin and the straps were loosed. Now, let's get out. Let's get out, let's get out. But I couldn't do it. I simply lift myself out of the cockpit. Arms and legs tried their best but it wasn't any use. A last desperate message was flashed upwards and this time it was marked 'Urgent'.

'Something else is holding us down,' it said. 'Something else, something else, something heavy.'

Still the arms and legs did not fight. They seemed to know instinctively that there was no point in using up their strength. They stayed quiet and waited for the answer, and oh what a time it took. Twenty, thirty, forty hot seconds. None of them really white hot yet, no sizzling of flesh or smell of burning meat, but that would come any moment now, because those old Gladiators aren't made of stressed steel like a Hurricane or a Spit. They have taut canvas wings, covered with magnificently inflammable dope, and underneath there are hundreds of small thin sticks, the kind you put under the logs for kindling, only these are drier and thinner. If a clever man said, 'I am going to build a big thing that will burn better and quicker than anything else in the world,' and if he applied himself diligently to his task, he would probably finish up by building something very like a Gladiator. I sat still waiting.

Then suddenly the reply, beautiful in its briefness, but at the same time explaining everything. 'Your – parachute – turn – the – buckle.'

I turned the buckle, released the parachute harness and with some effort hoisted myself up and tumbled over the side of the cockpit. Something seemed to be burning, so I rolled about a bit in the sand, then crawled away from the fire on all fours and lay down.

I heard some of my machine-gun ammunition going off in the heat and I heard some of the bullets thumping into the sand near by. I did not worry about them; I merely heard them.

Things were beginning to hurt. My face hurt most. There was something wrong with my face. Something had happened to it. Slowly I put up a hand to feel it. It was sticky. My nose didn't seem to be there. I tried to feel my teeth, but I cannot remember whether I came to any conclusion about them. I think I dozed off.

All of a sudden there was Peter. I heard his voice and I heard him dancing around and yelling like a madman and shaking my hand and saying, 'Jesus, I thought you were still inside. I came down half a mile away and ran like hell. Are you all right?'

I said, 'Peter, what has happened to my nose?'

I heard him striking a match in the dark. The night comes quickly in the desert. There was a pause.

'It actually doesn't seem to be there very much,' he said. 'Does it hurt?'

'Don't be a bloody fool, of course it hurts.'

He said he was going back to his machine to get some morphia out of his emergency pack, but he came back again soon, saying he couldn't find his aircraft in the dark.

'Peter,' I said, 'I can't see anything.'

'It's night,' he answered. 'I can't see either.'

It was cold now. It was bitter cold, and Peter lay down close alongside so that we could both keep a little warmer. Every now and then he would say, 'I've never seen a man without a nose before.' I kept spewing a lot of blood and every time I did it, Peter lit a match. Once he gave me a cigarette, but it got wet and I didn't want it anyway.

I do not know how long we stayed there and I remember only very little more. I remember that I kept telling Peter that there was a tin of sore throat tablets in my pocket, and that he should take one, otherwise he would catch my sore throat. I remember asking him where we were and him saying, 'We're between the two armies,' and then I remember English voices from an English patrol asking if we were Italians. Peter said something to them; I cannot remember what he said.

Later I remember hot thick soup and one spoonful making me sick. And all the time the pleasant feeling that Peter was around, being wonderful, doing wonderful things and never going away. That is all that I can remember.

The men stood beside the airplane painting away and talking about the heat.

'Painting pictures on the aircraft,' I said.

'Yes,' said Peter. 'It's a great idea. It's subtle.'

'Why?' I said. 'Just you tell me.'

'They're funny pictures,' he said. 'The German pilots will all laugh when they see them; they'll shake so with their laughing that they won't be able to shoot straight.'

'Oh baloney baloney baloney.'

'No, it's a great idea. It's fine. Come and have a look.'

We ran towards the line of aircraft. 'Hop, skip, jump,' said Peter. 'Hop skip jump, keep in time.'

'Hop skip jump,' I said, 'Hop skip jump,' and we danced along.

The painter on the first aeroplane had a straw hat on his head and a sad face. He was copying the drawing out of a magazine, and when Peter saw it he said, 'Boy oh boy look at that picture,' and he began to laugh. His laugh began with a rumble and grew quickly into a belly-roar and he slapped his thighs with his hands both at the same time and went on laughing with his body doubled up and his mouth wide open and his eyes shut. His silk top hat fell off his head on to the sand.

'That's not funny,' I said.

'Not funny!' he cried. 'What d'you mean "not funny"? Look at me. Look at me laughing. Laughing like this I couldn't hit anything. I couldn't hit a hay wagon or a house or a louse.' And he capered about on the sand, gurgling and shaking with laughter. Then he seized me by the arm and we danced over to the next aeroplane. 'Hop skip jump,' he said. 'Hop skip jump.'

There was a small man with a crumpled face writing a long story on the fuselage with a red crayon. His straw hat was perched right on the back of his head and his face was shiny with sweat.

'Good morning,' he said. 'Good morning, good morning,' and he swept his hat off his head in a very elegant way.

Peter said, 'Shut up,' and bent down and began to read what the little man had been writing. All the time Peter was spluttering and rumbling with laughter, and as he read he began to laugh afresh. He rocked from one side to the other and danced around on the sand slapping his thighs with his hands and bending his body. 'Oh my, what a story, what a story, what a story. Look at me. Look at me laughing,' and he hopped about on his toes, shaking his head and chortling like a madman. Then suddenly I saw the joke and I began to laugh with him. I laughed so much that my stomach hurt and I fell down and rolled around on the sand and roared and roared because it was so funny that there was nothing else I could do.

'Peter, you're marvellous,' I shouted. 'But can all those German pilots read English?'

'Oh hell,' he said. 'Oh hell. Stop,' he shouted. 'Stop your work,' and the painters all stopped their painting and turned round slowly and looked at Peter. They did a little caper on their toes and began to chant in unison. 'Rubbishy things – on all the wings, on all the wings, on all the wings,' they chanted.

'Shut up,' said Peter. 'We're in a jam. We must keep calm. Where's my top hat?'

'What?' I said.

'You can speak German,' he said. 'You must translate for us. He will translate for you,' he shouted to the painters. 'He will translate.'

Then I saw his black top hat lying in the sand. I looked away, then I looked around and saw it again. It was a silk opera hat and it was lying there on its side in the sand.

'You're mad,' I shouted. 'You're madder than hell. You don't know what you're doing. You'll get us all killed. You're absolutely plumb crazy, do you know that? You're crazier than hell. My God, you're crazy.'

'Goodness, what a noise you're making. You mustn't shout like that; it's not good for you.' This was a woman's voice. 'You've made yourself all hot,' she said, and I felt someone wiping my forehead with a handkerchief. 'You mustn't work yourself up like that.'

Then she was gone and I saw only the sky, which was pale blue. There were no clouds and all around were the German fighters. They were above, below and on every side and there was no way I could go; there was nothing I could do. They took it in turns to come in to attack and they flew their aircraft carelessly, banking and looping and dancing in the air. But I was not frightened, because of the funny pictures on my wings. I was confident and I thought, 'I am going to fight a hundred of them alone and I'll shoot them all down. I'll shoot them while they are laughing; that's what I'll do.'

Then they flew closer. The whole sky was full of them. There were so many that I did not know which ones to watch and which ones to attack. There were so many that they made a black curtain over the sky and only here and there could I see a little of the blue showing through. But there was enough to patch a Dutchman's trousers, which was all that mattered. So long as there was enough to do that, then everything was all right.

Still they flew closer. They came nearer and nearer, right up in front of my face so that I saw only the black crosses which stood out brightly against the colour of the Messerschmitts and against the blue of the sky; and as I turned my head quickly from one side to the other I saw more aircraft and more crosses and then I saw nothing but the arms of the crosses and the blue of the sky. The arms had hands and they joined together and made a circle and danced around my Gladiator, while the engines of the Messerschmitts sang joyfully in a deep voice. They were playing Oranges and Lemons and every now and then two would detach themselves and come out into the middle of the floor and make an attack and I knew then that it was Oranges and Lemons. They banked and swerved and danced upon their toes and they leant against the air first to one side, then to the other. 'Oranges and Lemons said the bells of St Clements,' sang the engines.

But I was still confident. I could dance better than they and I had a better partner. She was the most beautiful girl in the world. I looked down and saw the curve of her neck and the gentle slope of her pale shoulders and I saw her slender arms, eager and outstretched.

Suddenly I saw some bullet holes in my starboard wing and I got angry and scared both at the same time; but mostly I got angry. Then I got confident and I said, 'The German who did that had no sense of humour. There's always one man in a party who has no sense of humour. But there's nothing to worry about; there's nothing at all to worry about.'

Then I saw more bullet holes and I got scared. I slid back the hood of the cockpit and stood up and shouted, 'You fools, look at the funny pictures. Look at the one on my tail; look at the story on my fuselage. Please look at the story on my fuselage.'

But they kept on coming. They tripped into the middle of the floor in twos, shooting at me as they came. And the engines of the Messerschmitts sang loudly. 'When will you pay me, said the bells of Old Bailey?' sang the engines, and as they sang the black crosses danced and swayed to the rhythm of the music. There were more holes in my wings, in the engine cowling and in the cockpit.

Then suddenly there were some in my body.

But there was no pain, even when I went into a spin, when the wings of my plane went flip, flip, flip flip, faster and faster, when the blue sky and the black sea chased each other round and round until there was no longer any sky or sea but just the flashing of the sun as I turned. But the black crosses were following me down, still dancing and still holding hands and I could still hear the singing of their engines. 'Here comes a candle to light you to bed, here comes a chopper to chop off your head,' sang the engines.

Still the wings went flip flip, flip flip, and there was neither sky nor sea around me, but only the sun.

Then there was only the sea. I could see it below me and I could see the white horses, and I said to myself, 'Those are white horses riding a rough sea.' I knew then that my brain was going well because of the white horses and because of the sea. I knew that there was not much time because the sea and the white horses were nearer, the white horses were bigger and the sea was like a sea and like water, not like a smooth plate. Then there was only one white horse, rushing forward madly with his bit in his teeth, foaming at the mouth, scattering the spray with his hooves and arching his neck as he ran. He galloped on madly over the sea, riderless and uncontrollable, and I could tell that we were going to crash.

After that it was warmer, and there were no black crosses and there was no sky. But it was only warm because it was not hot and it was not cold. I was sitting in a great red chair made of velvet and it was evening. There was a wind blowing from behind.

'Where am I?' I said.

'You are missing. You are missing, believed killed.'

'Then I must tell my mother.'

'You can't. You can't use that phone.'

'Why not?'

'It goes only to God.'

'What did you say I was?'

'Missing, believed killed.'

'That's not true. It's a lie. It's a lousy lie because here I am and I'm not missing. You're just trying to frighten me and you won't succeed. You won't succeed, I tell you, because I know it's a lie and I'm going back to my squadron. You can't stop me because I'll just go. I'm going, you see, I'm going.'

I got up from the red chair and began to run.

'Let me see those X-rays again, nurse.'

'They're here, doctor.' This was the woman's voice again,

and now it came closer. 'You have been making a noise to-night, haven't you? Let me straighten your pillow for you, you're pushing it on to the floor.' The voice was close and it was very soft and nice.

'Am I missing?'

'No, of course not. You're fine.'

'They said I was missing.'

'Don't be silly; you're fine.'

Oh everyone's silly, silly, silly, but it was a lovely day, and I did not want to run but I couldn't stop. I kept on running across the grass and I couldn't stop because my legs were carrying me and I had no control over them. It was as if they did not belong to me, although when I looked down I saw that they were mine, that the shoes on the feet were mine and that the legs were joined to my body. But they would not do what I wanted; they just went on running across the field and I had to go with them. I ran and ran and ran, and although in some places the field was rough and bumpy, I never stumbled. I ran past trees and hedges and in one field there were some sheep which stopped their eating and scampered off as I ran past them. Once I saw my mother in a pale grey dress bending down picking mushrooms, and as I ran past she looked up and said, 'My basket's nearly full; shall we go home soon?' but my legs wouldn't stop and I had to go on.

Then I saw the cliff ahead and I saw how dark it was beyond the cliff. There was this great cliff and beyond it there was nothing but darkness, although the sun was shining in the field where I was running. The light of the sun stopped dead at the edge of the cliff and there was only darkness beyond. 'That must be where the night begins,' I thought, and once more I tried to stop but it was not any good. My legs began to go faster towards the cliff and they began to take longer strides, and I reached down with my hand and tried to stop them by clutching the cloth of my trousers, but it did not work; then I tried to fall down. But my legs were nimble, and each time I threw myself I landed on my toes and went on running.

Now the cliff and the darkness were much nearer and I could see that unless I stopped quickly I should go over the edge. Once more I tried to throw myself to the ground and once more I landed on my toes and went on running.

I was going fast as I came to the edge and I went straight on over it into the darkness and began to fall.

At first it was not quite dark. I could see little trees growing out of the face of the cliff, and I grabbed at them with my hands as I went down. Several times I managed to catch hold of a branch, but it always broke off at once because I was so heavy and because I was falling so fast, and once I caught a thick branch with both hands and the tree leaned forward and I heard the snapping of the roots one by one until it came away from the cliff and I went on falling. Then it became darker because the sun and the day were in the fields far away at the top of the cliff, and as I fell I kept my eyes open and watched the darkness turn from grey-black to black, from black to jet black and from jet black to pure liquid blackness which I could touch with my hands but which I could not see. But I went on falling, and it was so black that there was nothing anywhere and it was not any use doing anything or caring or thinking because of the blackness and because of the falling. It was not any use.

'You're better this morning. You're much better.' It was the woman's voice again.

'Hallo.'

'Hallo; we thought you were never going to get conscious.'

'Where am I?'

'In Alexandria; in hospital.'

'How long have I been here?'

'Four days.'

'What time is it?'

'Seven o'clock in the morning.'

'Why can't I see?'

I heard her walking a little closer.

'Oh, we've just put a bandage around your eyes for a bit.'

'How long for?'

'Just for a while. Don't worry. You're fine. You were very lucky, you know.'

I was feeling my face with my fingers but I couldn't feel it; I could only feel something else.

'What's wrong with my face?'

I heard her coming up to the side of my bed and I felt her hand touching my shoulder.

'You mustn't talk any more. You're not allowed to talk. It's bad for you. Just lie still and don't worry. You're fine.'

I heard the sound of her footsteps as she walked across the floor and I heard her open the door and shut it again.

'Nurse,' I said. 'Nurse.'

But she was gone.

Madame Rosette

'Oh Jesus, this is wonderful,' said the Stag.

He was lying back in the bath with a Scotch and soda in one hand and a cigarette in the other. The water was right up to the brim and he was keeping it warm by turning the tap with his toes.

He raised his head and took a little sip of his whisky, then he lay back and closed his eyes.

'For God's sake, get out,' said a voice from the next room. 'Come on, Stag, you've had over an hour.' Stuffy was sitting on the edge of the bed with no clothes on, drinking slowly and waiting his turn.

The Stag said, 'All right. I'm letting the water out now,' and he stretched out a leg and flipped up the plug with his toes.

Stuffy stood up and wandered into the bathroom holding his drink in his hand. The Stag lay in the bath for a few moments more, then, balancing his glass carefully on the soap rack, he stood up and reached for a towel. His body was short and square, with strong thick legs and exaggerated calf muscles. He had coarse curly ginger hair and a thin, rather pointed face covered with freckles. There was a layer of pale ginger hair on his chest.

'Jesus,' he said, looking down into the bathtub, 'I've brought half the desert with me.'

Stuffy said, 'Wash it out and let me get in. I haven't had a bath for five months.'

This was back in the early days when we were fighting the Italians in Libya. One flew very hard in those days because there were not many pilots. They certainly could not send any out from England because there they were fighting the Battle of Britain. So one remained for long periods out in the desert,

living the strange unnatural life of the desert, living in the
same dirty little tent, washing and shaving every day in a mug
full of one's own spat-out tooth water, all the time picking flies
out of one's tea and out of one's food, having sandstorms
which were as much in the tents as outside them so that placid
men became bloody-minded and lost their tempers with their
friends and with themselves; having dysentery and gippy
tummy and mastoid and desert sores, having some bombs from
the Italian S.79s, having no water and no women; having no
flowers growing out of the ground; having very little except
sand sand sand. One flew old Gloster Gladiators against the
Italian C.R.42s, and when one was not flying, it was difficult to
know what to do.

Occasionally one would catch scorpions, put them in empty
petrol cans and match them against each other in fierce mortal
combat. Always there would be a champion scorpion in the
squadron, a sort of Joe Louis who was invincible and won all
his fights. He would have a name; he would become famous
and his training diet would be a great secret known only to the
owner. Training diet was considered very important with
scorpions. Some were trained on corned beef, some on a thing
called Machonachies, which is an unpleasant canned meat
stew, some on live beetles and there were others who were
persuaded to take a little beer just before the fight, on the
premise that it made the scorpion happy and gave him confi-
dence. These last ones always lost. But there were great battles
and great champions, and in the afternoons when the flying
was over, one could often see a group of pilots and airmen
standing around in a circle on the sand, bending over with
their hands on their knees, watching the fight, exhorting the
scorpions and shouting at them as people shout at boxers or
wrestlers in a ring. Then there would be a victory, and the man
who owned the winner would become excited. He would dance
around in the sand yelling, waving his arms in the air and
extolling in a loud voice the virtues of the victorious animal.
The greatest scorpion of all was owned by a sergeant called
Wishful who fed him only on marmalade. The animal had an
unmentionable name, but he won forty-two consecutive fights

and then died quietly in training just when Wishful was considering the problem of retiring him to stud.

So you can see that because there were no great pleasures while living in the desert, the small pleasures became great pleasures and the pleasures of children became the pleasures of grown men. That was true for everyone; for the pilots, the fitters, the riggers, the corporals who cooked the food, and the men who kept the stores. It was true for the Stag and for Stuffy, so true that when the two of them wangled a forty-eight hour pass and a lift by air into Cairo, and when they got to the hotel, they were feeling about having a bath rather as you would feel on the first night of your honeymoon.

The Stag had dried himself and was lying on the bed with a towel round his waist, with his hands up behind his head, and Stuffy was in the bath, lying with his head against the back of the bath, groaning and sighing with ecstasy.

The Stag said, 'Stuffy.'

'Yes.'

'What are we going to do now?'

'Women.' said Stuffy. 'We must find some women to take out to supper.'

The Stag said, 'Later. That can wait till later.' It was early afternoon.

'I don't think it can wait,' said Stuffy.

'Yes,' said the Stag, 'it can wait.'

The Stag was very old and wise; he never rushed any fences. He was twenty-seven, much older than anyone else in the squadron, including the C.O., and his judgement was much respected by the others.

'Let's do a little shopping first,' he said.

'Then what?' said the voice from the bathroom.

'Then we can consider the other situation.'

There was a pause.

'Stag?'

'Yes.'

'Do you know any women here?'

'I used to. I used to know a Turkish girl with very white skin called Wenka, and a Yugoslav girl who was six inches taller than I, called Kiki, and another who I think was Syrian. I can't remember her name.'

'Ring them up,' said Stuffy.

'I've done it. I did it while you were getting the whisky. They've all gone. It isn't any good.'

'It's never any good,' Stuffy said.

The Stag said, 'We'll go shopping first. There is plenty of time.'

In an hour Stuffy got out of the bath. They both dressed themselves in clean khaki shorts and shirts and wandered downstairs, through the lobby of the hotel and out into the bright hot street. The Stag put on his sunglasses.

Stuffy said, 'I know. I want a pair of sunglasses.'

'All right. We'll go and buy some.'

They stopped a gharry, got in and told the driver to go to Cicurel's. Stuffy bought his sunglasses and the Stag bought some poker dice, then they wandered out again on to the hot crowded street.

'Did you see that girl?' said Stuffy.

'The one that sold us the sunglasses?'

'Yes. That dark one.'

'Probably Turkish,' said Stag.

Stuffy said, 'I don't care what she was. She was terrific. Didn't you think she was terrific?'

They were walking along the Sharia Kasr-el-Nil with their hands in their pockets, and Stuffy was wearing the sunglasses which he had just bought. It was a hot dusty afternoon, and the sidewalk was crowded with Egyptians and Arabs and small boys with bare feet. The flies followed the small boys and buzzed around their eyes, trying to get at the inflammation which was in them, which was there because their mothers had done something terrible to those eyes when the boys were young, so that they would not be eligible for military conscription when they grew older. The small boys pattered along beside the Stag and Stuffy shouting, 'Baksheesh, baksheesh,' in shrill insistent voices, and the flies followed the small boys. There was the smell of Cairo, which is not like the smell of any other city. It comes not from any one thing or from any one place; it comes from everything everywhere; from the gutters and the sidewalks, from the houses and the shops and the things in the shops and the food cooking in the shops, from the horses and the dung of the horses in the streets and from the drains; it comes from the people and the way the sun bears down upon the people and from the way the sun bears down upon the gutters and the drains and the horses and the food and the refuse in the streets. It is a rare, pungent smell, like something which is sweet and rotting and hot and salty and bitter all at the same time, and it is never absent, even in the cool of the early morning.

The two pilots walked along slowly among the crowd.

'Didn't you think she was terrific?' said Stuffy. He wanted to know what the Stag thought.

'She was all right.'

'Certainly she was all right. You know what, Stag?'

'What?'

'I would like to take that girl out tonight.'

They crossed over a street and walked on a little farther.

The Stag said, 'Well, why don't you? Why don't you ring up Rosette?'

'Who in the hell's Rosette?'

'Madame Rosette,' said the Stag. 'She is a great woman.'

They were passing a place called Tim's Bar. It was run by an Englishman called Tim Gilfillan who had been a quartermaster sergeant in the last war and who had somehow managed to get left behind in Cairo when the army went home.

'Tim's,' said the Stag. 'Let's go in.'

There was no one inside except for Tim, who was arranging his bottles on shelves behind the bar.

'Well, well, well,' he said, turning around. 'Where you boys been all this time?'

'Hello, Tim.'

He did not remember them, but he knew by their looks that they were in from the desert.

'How's my old friend Graziani?' he said, leaning his elbows on the counter.

'He's bloody close,' said the Stag. 'He's outside Mersah.'

'What you flying now?'

'Gladiators.'

'Hell, they had those here eight years ago.'

'Same ones still here,' said the Stag. 'They're clapped out.'
They got their whisky and carried the glasses over to a table in
the corner.

Stuffy said, 'Who's this Rosette?'

The Stag took a long drink and put down the glass.

'She's a great woman,' he said.

'Who is she?'

'She's a filthy old Syrian Jewess.'

'All right,' said Stuffy, 'all right, but what about her'

'Well,' said Stag, 'I'll tell you. Madame Rosette runs the
biggest brothel in the world. It is said that she can get you any
girl that you want in the whole of Cairo.'

'Bullshit.'

'No, it's true. You just ring her up and tell her where you
saw the woman, where she was working, what shop and at
which counter, together with an accurate description, and she
will do the rest.'

'Don't be such a bloody fool,' said Stuffy.

'It's true. It's absolutely true. Thirty-three squadron told me
about her.'

'They were pulling your leg.'

'All right. You go and look her up in the phone book.'

'She wouldn't be in the phone book under that name.'

'I'm telling you she is,' said Stag. 'Go and look her up under
Rosette. You'll see I'm right.'

Stuffy did not believe him, but he went over to Tim and
asked him for a telephone directory and brought it back to the
table. He opened it and turned the pages until he came to
R-o-s. He ran his finger down the column. Roseppi ... Rosery
... Rosette. There it was, Rosette, Madame and the address and
number, clearly printed in the book. The Stag was watching
him.

'Got it?' he said.

'Yes, here it is. Madame Rosette.'

'Well, why don't you go and ring her up?'

'What shall I say?'

The Stag looked down into his glass and poked the ice with his finger.

'Tell her you are a Colonel,' he said. 'Colonel Higgins; she mistrusts pilot officers. And tell her that you have seen a beautiful dark girl selling sunglasses at Cicurel's and that you would like, as you put it, to take her out to dinner.'

'There isn't a telephone here.'

'Oh yes there is. There's one over there.'

Stuffy looked around and saw the telephone on the wall at the end of the bar.

'I haven't got a piastre piece.'

'Well, I have,' said Stag. He fished in his pocket and put a piastre on the table.

'Tim will hear everything I say.'

'What the hell does that matter? He probably rings her up himself. You're windy,' he added.

'You're a shit,' said Stuffy.

Stuffy was just a child. He was nineteen; seven whole years younger than the Stag. He was fairly tall and he was thin, with a lot of black hair and a handsome wide-mouthed face which was coffee brown from the sun of the desert. He was unquestionably the finest pilot in the squadron, and already in these early days, his score was fourteen Italians confirmed destroyed. On the ground he moved slowly and lazily like a tired person and he thought slowly and lazily like a sleepy child, but when he was up in the air his mind was quick and his movements were quick, so quick that they were like reflex actions. It seemed, when he was on the ground, almost as though he was resting, as though he was dozing a little in order to make sure that when he got into the cockpit he would wake up fresh and quick, ready for that two hours of high concentration. But Stuffy was away from the aerodrome now and he had something on his mind which had waked him up almost like flying. It might not last, but for the moment anyway, he was concentrating.

He looked again in the book for the number, got up and

walked slowly over to the telephone. He put in the piastre, dialled the number and heard it ringing the other end. The Stag was sitting at the table looking at him and Tim was still behind the bar arranging his bottles. Tim was only about five yards away and he was obviously going to listen to everything that was said. Stuffy felt rather foolish. He leaned against the bar and waited, hoping that no one would answer.

Then click, the receiver was lifted at the other end and he heard a woman's voice saying, 'Allo'.

He said, 'Hello, is Madame Rosette there?' He was watching Tim. Tim went on arranging his bottles, pretending to take no notice, but Stuffy knew that he was listening.

'This ees Madame Rosette. Oo ees it?' Her voice was petulant and gritty. She sounded as if she did not want to be bothered with anyone just then.

Stuffy tried to sound casual. 'This is Colonel Higgins.'

'Colonel oo?'

'Colonel Higgins.' He spelled it.

'Yes, Colonel. What do you want?' She sounded impatient. Obviously this was a woman who stood no nonsense. He still tried to sound casual.

'Well, Madame Rosette, I was wondering if you could help me over a little matter.'

Stuffy was watching Tim. He was listening all right. You can always tell if someone is listening when he is pretending not to. He is careful not to make any noise about what he is doing and he pretends that he is concentrating very hard upon his job. Tim was like that now, moving the bottles quickly from one shelf to another, watching the bottles, making no noise, never looking around into the room. Over in the far corner the Stag was leaning forward with his elbows on the table, smoking a cigarette. He was watching Stuffy, enjoying the whole business and knowing that Stuffy was embarrassed because of Tim. Stuffy had to go on.

'I was wondering if you could help me,' he said. 'I was in Cicurel's today buying a pair of sunglasses and I saw a girl there whom I would very much like to take out to dinner.'

'What's 'er name?' The hard, rasping voice was more business-like than ever.

'I don't know,' he said sheepishly.

'What's she look like?'

'Well, she's got dark hair, and tall and, well, she's very beautiful.'

'What sort of dress was she wearing?'

'Er, let me see. I think it was a kind of white dress with red flowers printed all over it.' Then, as a brilliant afterthought, he added, 'She had a red belt.' He remembered that she had been wearing a shiny red belt.

There was a pause. Stuffy watched Tim who wasn't making any noise with the bottles; he was picking them up carefully and putting them down carefully.

Then the loud gritty voice again, 'It may cost you a lot.'

'That's all right.' Suddenly he didn't like the conversation any more. He wanted to finish it and get away.

'Might cost you six pounds, might cost you eight or ten. I don't know till I've seen her. That all right?'

'Yes yes, that's all right.'

'Where you living, Colonel?'

'Metropolitan Hotel,' he said without thinking.

'All right, I give you a ring later.' And she put down the receiver, bang.

Stuffy hung up, went slowly back to the table and sat down.

'Well,' said Stag, 'that was all right, wasn't it?'

'Yes, I suppose so.'

'What did she say?'

'She said that she would call me back at the hotel.'

'You mean she'll call Colonel Higgins at the hotel.'

Stuffy said, 'Oh Christ.'

Stag said, 'It's all right. We'll tell the desk that the Colonel is in our room and to put his calls through to us. What else did she say?'

'She said it may cost me a lot, six or ten pounds.'

'Rosette will take ninety per cent of it,' said Stag. 'She's a filthy old Syrian Jewess.'

'How will she work it?' Stuffy said.

He was really a gentle person and now he was feeling worried about having started something which might become complicated.

'Well,' said Stag, 'she'll dispatch one of her pimps to locate the girl and find out who she is. If she's already on the books, then it's easy. If she isn't, the pimp will proposition her there and then over the counter at Cicurel's. If the girl tells him to go to hell, he'll up the price, and if she still tells him to go to hell, he'll up the price still more, and in the end she'll be tempted by the cash and probably agree. Then Rosette quotes you a price three times as high and takes the balance herself. You have to pay her, not the girl. Of course, after that the girl goes on Rosette's books, and once she's in her clutches she's finished. Next time Rosette will dictate the price and the girl will not be in a position to argue.'

'Why?'

'Because if she refuses, Rosette will say, "All right, my girl, I shall see that your employers, that's Cicurel's, are told about what you did last time, how you've been working for me and using their shop as a market place. Then they'll fire you." That's what Rosette will say, and the wretched girl will be frightened and do what she's told.'

Stuffy said, 'Sounds like a nice person.'

'Who?'

'Madame Rosette.'

'Charming,' said Stag. 'She's a charming person.'

It was hot. Stuffy wiped his face with his handkerchief.

'More whisky,' said Stag. 'Hi, Tim, two more of those.'

Tim brought the glasses over and put them on the table without saying anything. He picked up the empty glasses and went away at once. To Stuffy it seemed as though he was different from what he had been when they first came in. He wasn't cheery any more, he was quiet and offhand. There wasn't any more 'Hi, you fellows, where you been all this time' about him now, and when he got back behind the counter he turned his back and went on arranging the bottles.

The Stag said, 'How much money you got?'

'Nine pounds, I think.'

'May not be enough. You gave her a free hand, you know. You ought to have set a limit. She'll sting you now.'

'I know,' Stuffy said.

They went on drinking for a little while without talking. Then Stag said, 'What you worrying about, Stuffy?'

'Nothing,' he answered. 'Nothing at all. Let's go back to the hotel. She may ring up.'

They paid for their drinks and said good-bye to Tim, who nodded but didn't say anything. They went back to the Metropolitan and as they went past the desk, the Stag said to the clerk, 'If a call comes in for Colonel Higgins, put it through to our room. He'll be there.' The Egyptian said, 'Yes, sir,' and made a note of it.

In the bedroom, the Stag lay down on his bed and lit a cigarette. 'And what am I going to do tonight?' he said.

Stuffy had been quiet all the way back to the hotel. He hadn't said a word. Now he sat down on the edge of the other bed with his hands still in his pockets and said, 'Look, Stag, I'm not very keen on this Rosette deal any more. It may cost too much. Can't we put it off?'

The Stag sat up. 'Hell no,' he said. 'You're committed. You can't fool about with Rosette like that. She's probably working on it at this moment. You can't back out now.'

'I may not be able to afford it,' Stuffy said.

'Well, wait and see.'

Stuffy got up, went over to the parachute bag and took out the bottle of whisky. He poured out two, filled the glasses with water from the tap in the bathroom, came back and gave one to the Stag.

'Stag,' he said. 'Ring up Rosette and tell her that Colonel Higgins has had to leave town urgently, to rejoin his regiment in the desert. Ring her up and tell her that. Say the Colonel asked you to deliver the message because he didn't have time.'

'Ring her up yourself.'

'She'd recognize my voice. Come on, Stag, you ring her.'

'No,' he said, 'I won't.'

'Listen,' said Stuffy suddenly. It was the child Stuffy speaking. 'I don't want to go out with that woman and I don't want to have any dealings with Madame Rosette tonight. We can think of something else.'

The Stag looked up quickly. Then he said, 'All right. I'll ring her.'

He reached for the phone book, looked up her number and spoke it into the telephone. Stuffy heard him get her on the line and he heard him giving her the message from the Colonel. There was a pause, then the Stag said, 'I'm sorry Madame Rosette, but it's nothing to do with me. I'm merely delivering a message.' Another pause; then the Stag said the same thing over again and that went on for quite a long time, until he must have got tired of it, because in the end he put down the receiver and lay back on his bed. He was roaring with laughter.

'The lousy old bitch,' he said, and he laughed some more.

Stuffy said, 'Was she angry?'

'Angry,' said Stag. 'Was she angry? You should have heard her. Wanted to know the Colonel's regiment and God knows what else and said he'd have to pay. She said you boys think you can fool around with me but you can't.'

'Hooray,' said Stuffy. 'The filthy old Jewess.'

'Now what are we going to do?' said the Stag. 'It's six o'clock already.'

'Let's go out and do a little drinking in some of those Gyppi places.'

'Fine. We'll do a Gyppi pub crawl.'

They had one more drink, then they went out. They went to a place called the Excelsior, then they went to a place called the Sphinx, then to a small place called by an Egyptian name, and by ten o'clock they were sitting happily in a place which hadn't got a name at all, drinking beer and watching a kind of stage show. At the Sphinx they had picked up a pilot from Thirty-three squadron, who said that his name was William. He was about the same age as Stuffy, but his face was younger, for he had not been flying so long. It was especially around his mouth that he was younger. He had a round schoolboy face and a small turned-up nose and his skin was brown from the desert.

The three of them sat happily in the place without a name drinking beer, because beer was the only thing that they served there. It was a long wooden room with an unpolished wooden sawdust floor and wooden tables and chairs. At the far end there was a raised wooden stage where there was a show going on. The room was full of Egyptians, sitting drinking black coffee with the red tarbooshes on their heads. There were two fat girls on the stage dressed in shiny silver pants and silver brassieres. One was waggling her bottom in time to the music. The other was waggling her bosom in time to the music. The bosom waggler was most skilful. She could waggle one bosom without waggling the other and sometimes she would waggle her bottom as well. The Egyptians were spellbound and kept giving her a big hand. The more they clapped the more she waggled and the more she waggled the faster the music played, and the faster the music played, the faster she waggled, faster and faster and faster, never losing the tempo, never losing the fixed brassy smile that was upon her face, and the Egyptians clapped more and more and louder and louder as the speed increased. Everyone was very happy.

When it was over William said, 'Why do they always have those dreary fat women? Why don't they have beautiful women?'

The Stag said, 'The Gyppies like them fat. They like them like that.'

'Impossible,' said Stuffy.

'It's true,' Stag said. 'It's an old business. It comes from the days when there used to be lots of famines here, and all the poor people were thin and all the rich people and the aristocracy were well fed and fat. If you got someone fat you couldn't go wrong; she was bound to be high-class.'

'Bullshit,' said Stuffy.

William said, 'Well, we'll soon find out. I'm going to ask those Gyppies.' He jerked his thumb towards two middle-aged Egyptians who were sitting at the next table, only about four feet away.

'No,' said Stag. 'No, William. We don't want them over here.'

'Yes,' said Stuffy.

'Yes,' said William. 'We've got to find out why the Gyppies like fat woman.'

He was not drunk. None of them was drunk, but they were happy with a fair amount of beer and whisky, and William was the happiest. His brown schoolboy face was radiant with happiness, his turned-up nose seemed to have turned up a little more, and he was probably relaxing for the first time in many weeks. He got up, took three paces over to the table of the Egyptians and stood in front of them, smiling.

'Gentlemen,' he said, 'my friends and I would be honoured if you would join us at our table.'

The Egyptians had dark greasy skins and podgy faces. They were wearing the red hats and one of them had a gold tooth. At first, when William addressed them, they looked a little alarmed. Then they caught on, looked at each other, grinned and nodded.

'Pleess,' said one.

'Pleess,' said the other, and they got up, shook hands with William and followed him over to where the Stag and Stuffy were sitting.

William said, 'Meet my friends. This is the Stag. This is Stuffy. I am William.'

The Stag and Stuffy stood up, they all shook hands, the Egyptians said 'Pleess' once more and then everyone sat down.

The Stag knew that their religion forbade them to drink. 'Have a coffee,' he said.

The one with the gold tooth grinned broadly, raised his palms upward and hunched his shoulders a little. 'For me,' he said, 'I am accustomed. But for my frient,' and he spread out his hands towards the other, 'for my frient – I cannot speak.'

The Stag looked at the friend. 'Coffee?' he asked.

'Pleess,' he answered. 'I am accustomed.'

'Good,' said Stag. 'Two coffees.'

He called a waiter. 'Two coffees,' he said. 'And, wait a minute. Stuffy, William, more beer?'

'For me,' Stuffy said, 'I am accustomed. But for my friend,'

65

and he turned towards William, 'for my friend – I cannot speak.'

William said, 'Please. I am accustomed.' None of them smiled.

The Stag said, 'Good. Waiter, two coffees and three beers.' The waiter fetched the order and the Stag paid. The Stag lifted his glass towards the Egyptians and said, 'Bung ho.'

'Bung ho,' said Stuffy.

'Bung ho,' said William.

The Egyptians seemed to understand and they lifted their coffee cups. 'Pleess,' said the one. 'Thank you,' said the other. They drank.

The Stag put down his glass and said, 'It is an honour to be in your country.'

'You like?'

'Yes,' said the Stag. 'Very fine.'

The music had started again and the two fat women in silver tights were doing an encore. The encore was a knockout. It was surely the most remarkable exhibition of muscle control that has ever been witnessed; for although the bottom-waggler was still just waggling her bottom, the bosom-waggler was standing like an oak tree in the centre of the stage with her arms above her head. Her left bosom she was rotating in a clockwise direction and her right bosom in an anticlockwise direction. At the same time she was waggling her bottom and it was all in time to the music. Gradually the music increased its speed, and as it got faster, the rotating and the waggling got faster and some of the Egyptians were so spellbound by the contra-rotating bosoms of the woman that they were unconsciously following the movements of the bosoms with their hands, holding their hands up in front of them and describing circles in the air. Everyone stamped their feet and screamed with delight and the two women on the stage continued to smile their fixed brassy smiles.

Then it was over. The applause gradually died down.

'Remarkable,' said the Stag.

'You like?'

'Please, it was remarkable.'

'Those girls,' said the one with the gold tooth, 'very special.'

William couldn't wait any longer. He leaned across the table and said, 'Might I ask you a question?'

'Pleess,' said Golden Tooth. 'Pleess.'

'Well,' said William, 'How do you like your women? Like this – slim?' and he demonstrated with his hands. 'Or like this – fat?'

The gold tooth shone brightly behind a big grin. 'For me, I like like this, fat,' and a pair of podgy hands drew a big circle in the air.

'And your friend?' said William.

'For my frient,' he answered, 'I cannot speak.'

'Pleess,' said the friend. 'Like this.' He grinned and drew a fat girl in the air with his hands.

Stuffy said, 'Why do you like them fat?'

Golden Tooth thought for a moment, then he said, 'You like them slim, eh?'

'Please,' said Stuffy. 'I like them slim.'

'Why you like them slim? You tell me.'

Stuffy rubbed the back of his neck with the palm of his hand. 'William,' he said, 'why do we like them slim?'

'For me,' said William, 'I am accustomed.'

'So am I,' Stuffy said. 'But why?'

William considered. 'I don't know,' he said. 'I don't know why we like them slim.'

'Ha,' said Golden Tooth, 'You don't know.' He leaned over the table towards William and said triumphantly, 'And me, I do not know either.'

But that wasn't good enough for William. 'The Stag,' he said, 'says that all rich people in Egypt used to be fat and all poor people were thin.'

'No,' said Golden Tooth, 'No no no. Look those girls up there. Very fat; very poor. Look queen of Egypt, Queen Farida. Very thin; very rich. Quite wrong.'

'Yes, but what about years ago?' said William.

'What is this, years ago?'

William said, 'Oh all right. Let's leave it.'

The Egyptians drank their coffee and made noises like the

last bit of water running out of the bathtub. When they had finished, they got up to go.

'Going?' said the Stag.

'Pleess,' said Golden Tooth.

William said, 'Thank you.' Stuffy said, 'Pleess.' the other Egyptian said, 'Pleess' and the Stag said, 'Thank you.' They all shook hands and the Egyptians departed.

'Ropey types,' said William.

'Very,' said Stuffy. 'Very ropey types.'

The three of them sat on drinking happily until midnight, when the waiter came up and told them that the place was closing and that there were no more drinks. They were still not really drunk because they had been taking it slowly, but they were feeling healthy.

'He says we've got to go.'

'All right. Where shall we go? Where shall we go, Stag?'

'I don't know. Where do you want to go?'

'Let's go to another place like this,' said William. 'This is a fine place.'

There was a pause. Stuffy was stroking the back of his neck with his hand. 'Stag,' he said slowly, 'I know where I want to go. I want to go to Madame Rosette's and I want to rescue all the girls there.'

'Who's Madame Rosette?' William said.

'She's a great woman,' said the Stag.

'She's a filthy old Syrian Jewess,' said Stuffy.

'She's a lousy old bitch,' said the Stag.

'All right,' said William. 'Let's go. But who is she?'

They told him who she was. They told him about their telephone calls and about Colonel Higgins, and William said, 'Come on, let's go. Let's go and rescue all the girls.'

They got up and left. When they went outside, they remembered that they were in a rather remote part of the town.

'We'll have to walk a bit,' said Stag. 'No gharries here.'

It was a dark starry night with no moon. The street was narrow and blacked-out. It smelled strongly with the smell of Cairo. It was quiet as they walked along, and now and again they passed a man or sometimes two men standing back in the shadow of a house, leaning against the wall of the house, smoking.

'I say,' said William, 'ropey, what?'

'Very,' said Stuffy. 'Very bad types.'

They walked on, the three of them walking abreast; square short ginger-haired Stag, tall dark Stuffy, and tall young William who went barehead because he had lost his cap. They headed roughly towards the centre of the town where they knew that they would find a gharry to take them on to Rosette.

Stuffy said, 'Oh, won't the girls be pleased when we rescue them?'

'Jesus,' said the Stag, 'it ought to be a party.'

'Does she actually keep them locked up?' William said.

'Well, no,' said Stag. 'Not exactly. But if we rescue them now, they won't have to work any more tonight anyway. You see, the girls she has at her place are nothing but ordinary shop girls who still work during the day in the shops. They have all of them made some mistake or other which Rosette either engineered or found out about, and now she has put the screws on them; she makes them come along in the evening. But they hate her and they do not depend on her for a living. They would kick her in the teeth if they got the chance.'

Stuffy said, 'We'll give them the chance.'

They crossed over a street. William said, 'How many girls will there be there, Stag?'

'I don't know. I suppose there might be thirty.'

'Good God,' said William. 'This *will* be a party. Does she really treat them very badly?'

The Stag said, 'Thirty-three squadron told me that she pays them nothing, about twenty akkers a night. She charges the customers a hundred or two hundred akkers each. Every girl earns for Rosette between five hundred and a thousand akkers every night.'

'Good God,' said William. 'A thousand piastres a night and thirty girls. She must be a millionaire.'

'She is. Someone calculated that not even counting her outside business, she makes the equivalent of about fifteen hundred pounds a week. That's, let me see, that's between five and six thousand pounds a month. Sixty thousand pounds a year.'

Stuffy came out of his dream. 'Jesus,' he said, 'Jesus Christ. The filthy old Syrian Jewess.'

'The lousy old bitch,' said William.

They were coming into a more civilized section of the town, but still there were no gharries.

The Stag said, 'Did you hear about Mary's House?'

'What's Mary's House?' said William.

'It's a place in Alexandria. Mary is the Rosette of Alex.'

'Lousy old bitch,' said William.

'No,' Stag said. 'They say she's a good woman. But anyway, Mary's House was hit by a bomb last week. The navy was in port at the time and the place was full of sailors, nautic types.'

'Killed?'

'Lots of them killed. And d'you know what happened? They posted them as killed in action.'

'The Admiral is a gentleman,' said Stuffy.

'Magnificent,' said William.

Then they saw a gharry and hailed it.

Stuffy said, 'We don't know the address.'

'He'll know it,' said Stag. 'Madame Rosette,' he said to the driver.

The driver grinned and nodded. Then William said, 'I'm going to drive. Give me the reins, driver, and sit up here beside me and tell me where to go.'

The driver protested vigorously, but when William gave him ten piastres, he gave him the reins. William sat high up on the driver's seat with the driver beside him. The Stag and Stuffy got in the back of the carriage.

'Take off,' said Stuffy. William took off. The horses began to gallop.

'No good,' shrieked the driver. 'No good. Stop.'

'Which way Rosette?' shouted William.

'Stop,' shrieked the driver.

William was happy. 'Rosette,' he shouted. 'Which way?'

The driver made a decision. He decided that the only way to stop this madman was to get him to his destination. 'This way,' he shrieked. 'Left.' William pulled hard on the left rein and the horses swerved around the corner. The gharry took it on one wheel.

'Too much bank,' shouted Stuffy from the back seat.

'Which way now?' shouted William.

'Left,' shrieked the driver. They took the next street to the left, then they took one to the right, two more to the left, then one to the right again and suddenly the driver yelled, 'Here pleess, here Rosette. Stop.'

William pulled hard on the reins and gradually the horses raised their heads with the pulling and slowed down to a trot.

'Where?' said William.

'Here,' said the driver. 'Pleess.' He pointed to a house twenty yards ahead. William brought the horses to a stop right in front of it.

'Nice work, William,' said Stuffy.

'Jesus,' said the Stag. 'That was quick.'

'Marvellous,' said William. 'Wasn't it?' He was very happy.

The driver was sweating through his shirt and he was too frightened to be angry.

William said, 'How much?'

'Pleess, twenty piastres.'

William gave him forty and said, 'Thank you very much. Fine horses.' The little man took the money, jumped up on to the gharry, and drove off. He was in a hurry to get away.

They were in another of those narrow, dark streets, but the houses, what they could see of them, looked huge and prosperous. The one which the driver had said was Rosette's was wide and thick and three storeys high, built of grey concrete, and it had a large thick front door which stood wide open. As they went in, the Stag said, 'Now leave this to me. I've got a plan.'

Inside there was a cold grey dusty stone hall, lit by a bare electric light bulb in the ceiling, and there was a man standing in the hall. He was a mountain of a man, a huge Egyptian with a flat face and two cauliflower ears. In his wrestling days he had probably been billed as Abdul the Killer or The

Poisonous Pasha, but now he wore a dirty white cotton suit.

The Stag said, 'Good evening. Is Madame Rosette here?'

Abdul looked hard at the three pilots, hesitated, then said, 'Madame Rosette top floor.'

'Thank you,' said Stag. 'Thank you very much.' Stuffy noticed that the Stag was being polite. There was always trouble for somebody when he was like that. Back in the squadron, when he was leading a flight, when they sighted the enemy and when there was going to be a battle, the Stag never gave an order without saying 'Please' and he never received a message without saying 'Thank you'. He was saying 'Thank you' now to Abdul.

They went up the bare stone steps which had iron railings. They went past the first landing and the second landing, and the place was as bare as a cave. At the top of the third flight of steps, there was no landing; it was walled off, and the stairs ran up to a door. The Stag pressed the bell. They waited a while, then a little panel in the door slid back and a pair of small black eyes peeked through. A woman's voice said, 'What you boys want?' Both the Stag and Stuffy recognized the voice from the telephone. The Stag said, 'We would like to see Madame Rosette.' He pronounced the Madame in the French way because he was being polite.

'You officers? Only officers here,' said the voice. She had a voice like a broken board.

'Yes,' said Stag. 'We are officers.'

'You don't look like officers. What kind of officers?'

'R.A.F.'

There was a pause. The Stag knew that she was considering. She had probably had trouble with pilots before, and he hoped only that she would not see William and the light that was dancing in his eyes; for William was still feeling the way he had felt when he drove the gharry. Suddenly the panel closed and the door opened.

'All right, come in,' she said. She was too greedy, this woman, even to pick her customers carefully.

They went in and there she was. Short, fat, greasy, with wisps of untidy black hair straggling over her forehead; a large, mud-coloured face, a large wide nose and a small fish mouth, with just the trace of a black moustache above the mouth. She had on a loose black satin dress.

'Come into the office, boys,' she said, and started to waddle down the passage to the left. It was a long wide passage, about fifty yards long and four or five yards wide. It ran through the middle of the house, parallel with the street, and as you came in from the stairs, you had to turn left along it. All the way down there were doors, about eight or ten of them on each side. If you turned right as you came in from the stairs, you ran into the end of the passage, but there was one door there too, and as the three of them walked in, they heard a babble of female voices from behind that door. The Stag noted that it was the girls' dressing room.

'This way, boys,' said Rosette. She turned left and slopped down the passage, away from the door with the voices. The three followed her, Stag first, then Stuffy, then William, down the passage which had a red carpet on the floor and huge pink lampshades hanging from the ceiling. They got about halfway down the passage when there was a yell from the dressing room behind them. Rosette stopped and looked around.

'You go on, boys,' she said, 'into the office, last door on the left. I won't be a minute.' She turned and went back towards the dressing-room door. They didn't go on. They stood and watched her, and just as she got to the door, it opened and a girl rushed out. From where they stood, they could see that her fair hair was all over her face and that she had on an untidy-looking green evening dress. She saw Rosette in front of her and she stopped. They heard Rosette say something, something angry and quick spoken, and they heard the girl shout something back at her. They saw Rosette raise her right arm and they saw her hit the girl smack on the side of the face with the palm of her hand. They saw her draw back her hand and hit her again in the same place. She hit her hard. The girl put her hands up to her face and began to cry. Rosette opened the door of the dressing room and pushed her back inside.

'Jesus,' said the Stag. 'She's tough.' William said, 'So am I.' Stuffy didn't say anything.

Rosette came back to them and said, 'Come along, boys. Just a bit of trouble, that's all.' She led them to the end of the passage and in through the last door on the left. This was the office. It was a medium-sized room with two red plush sofas, two or three red plush armchairs and a thick red carpet on the floor. In one corner was a small desk, and Rosette sat herself behind it, facing the room.

'Sit down, boys,' she said.

The Stag took an armchair, Stuffy and William sat on a sofa.

'Well,' she said, and her voice became sharp and urgent. 'Let's do business.'

The Stag leaned forward in his chair. His short ginger hair looked somehow wrong against the bright red plush. 'Madame Rosette,' he said, 'it is a great pleasure to meet you. We have heard so much about you.' Stuffy looked at the Stag. He was being polite again. Rosette looked at him too, and her little black eyes were suspicious. 'Believe me,' the Stag went on, 'we've really been looking forward to this for quite a time now.'

His voice was so pleasant and he was so polite that Rosette took it.

'That's nice of you boys,' she said. 'You'll always have a good time here. I see to that. Now – business.'

William couldn't wait any longer. He said slowly, 'The Stag says that you're a great woman.'

'Thanks, boys.'

Stuffy said, 'The Stag says that you're a filthy old Syrian Jewess.'

William said quickly, 'The Stag says that you're a lousy old bitch.'

'And I know what I'm talking about,' said the Stag.

Rosette jumped to her feet. 'What's this?' she shrieked, and her face was no longer the colour of mud; it was the colour of red clay. The men did not move. They did not smile or laugh; they sat quite still, leaning forward a little in their seats, watching her.

Rosette had had trouble before, plenty of it, and she knew

how to deal with it. But this was different. They didn't seem drunk, it wasn't about money and it wasn't about one of her girls. It was about herself and she didn't like it.

'Get out,' she yelled. 'Get out unless you want trouble.' But they did not move.

For a moment she paused, then she stepped quickly from behind her desk and made for the door. But the Stag was there first and when she went for him, Stuffy and William each caught one of her arms from behind.

'We'll lock her in,' said the Stag. 'Let's get out.'

Then she really started yelling and the words which she used cannot be written down on paper, for they were terrible words. They poured out of her small fish mouth in one long unbroken high-pitched stream, and little bits of spit and saliva came out with them. Stuffy and William pulled her back by the arms towards one of the big chairs and she fought and yelled like a large fat pig being dragged to the slaughter. They got her in front of the chair and gave her a quick push so that she fell backwards into it. Stuffy nipped across to her desk, bent down quickly and jerked the telephone cord from its connection. The Stag had the door open and all three of them were out of the room before Rosette had time to get up. The Stag had taken the key from the inside of the door, and now he locked it. The three of them stood outside in the passage.

'Jesus,' said the Stag. 'What a woman!'

'Mad as hell,' William said. 'Listen to her.'

They stood outside in the passage and they listened. They heard her yelling, then she began banging on the door, but she went on yelling and her voice was not the voice of a woman, it was the voice of an enraged but articulate bull.

The Stag said, 'Now quick. The girls. Follow me. And from now on you've got to act serious. You've got to act serious as hell.'

He ran down the passage towards the dressing room, followed by Stuffy and William. Outside the door he stopped, the other two stopped and they could still hear Rosette yelling from her office. The Stag said, 'Now don't say anything. Just act serious as hell,' and he opened the door and went in.

There were about a dozen girls in the room. They all looked up. They stopped talking and looked up at the Stag, who was standing in the doorway. The Stag clicked his heels and said, 'This is the Military Police. *Les Gendarmes Militaires.*' He said it in a stern voice and with a straight face and he was standing there in the doorway at attention with his cap on his head. Stuffy and William stood behind him.

'This is the Military Police,' he said again, and he produced his identification card and held it up between two fingers.

The girls didn't move or say anything. They stayed still in the middle of what they were doing and they were like a tableau because they stayed so still. One had been pulling on a stocking and she stayed like that, sitting on a chair with her leg out straight and the stocking up to her knee with her hands on the stocking. One had been doing her hair in front of a mirror and when she looked round she kept her hands up to her hair. One was standing up and had been applying lipstick and she raised her eyes to the Stag but still held the lipstick to her mouth. Several were just sitting around on plain wooden chairs, doing nothing, and they raised their heads and turned them to the door, but they went on sitting. Most of them were in some sort of shiny evening dress, one or two were half-clothed, but most of them were in shiny green or shiny blue or shiny red or shiny gold, and when they turned to look at the Stag, they were so still that they were like a tableau.

The Stag paused. Then he said, 'I am to state on behalf of the authorities that they are sorry to disturb you. My apologies, mesd'moiselles. But it is necessary that you come with us for purposes of registration, et cetera. Afterwards you will be allowed to go. It is a mere formality. But now you must come, please. I have conversed with Madame.'

The Stag stopped speaking, but still the girls did not move.

'Please,' said the Stag, 'get your coats. We are the military.' He stepped aside and held open the door. Suddenly the tableau dissolved, the girls got up, puzzled and murmuring, and two or three of them moved towards the door. The others followed. The ones that were half-clothed quickly slipped into dresses, patted their hair with their hands and came too. None of them had coats.

'Count them,' said the Stag to Stuffy as they filed out of the door. Stuffy counted them aloud and there were fourteen.

'Fourteen, sir,' said Stuffy, who was trying to talk like a sergeant-major.

The Stag said, 'Correct,' and he turned to the girls who were crowded in the passage. 'Now, mesd'moiselles, I have the list of your names from Madame, so please do not try to run away. And do not worry. This is merely a formality of the military.'

William was out in the passage opening the door which led to the stairs, and he went out first. The girls followed and the Stag and Stuffy brought up the rear. The girls were quiet and puzzled and worried and a little frightened and they didn't talk, none of them talked except for a tall one with black hair who said, 'Mon Dieu, a formality of the military. Mon Dieu, mon Dieu, what next.' But that was all and they went on down. In the hall they met the Egyptian who had a flat face and two cauliflower ears. For a moment it looked as though there would be trouble. But the Stag waved his identification card in his face and said, 'The Military Police,' and the man was so surprised that he did nothing and let them pass.

And so they came out into the street and the Stag said, 'It is necessary to walk a little way, but only a very little way,' and they turned right and walked along the sidewalk with the Stag leading, Stuffy at the rear and William walking out on the road guarding the flank. There was some moon now. One could see quite well and William tried to keep in step with Stag and Stuffy tried to keep in step with William, and they swung their arms and held their heads up high and looked very military, and the whole thing was a sight to behold. Fourteen girls in shiny evening dresses, fourteen girls in the moonlight in shiny green, shiny blue, shiny red, shiny black and shiny gold, marching along the street with the Stag in front, William alongside and Stuffy at the rear. It was a sight to behold.

The girls had started chattering. The Stag could hear them, although he didn't look around. He marched on at the head of the column and when they came to the crossroads he turned right. The others followed and they had walked fifty yards down the block when they came to an Egyptian café. The Stag saw it and he saw the lights burning behind the blackout curtains. He turned around and shouted 'Halt!' The girls stopped, but they went on chattering and anyone could see that there was mutiny in the ranks. You can't make fourteen girls in high heels and shiny evening dresses march all over town with you at night, not for long anyway, not for long, even if it is a formality of the military. The Stag knew it and now he was speaking.

'Mesd'moiselles,' he said, 'listen to me.' But there was mutiny in the ranks and they went on talking and the tall one with dark hair was saying, 'Mon Dieu, what is this? What in hell's name sort of a thing is this, oh mon Dieu?'

'Quiet,' said the Stag. 'Quiet!' and the second time he shouted it as a command. The talking stopped.

'Mesd'moiselles,' he said, and now he became polite. He talked to them in his best way and when the Stag was polite there wasn't anyone who didn't take it. It was an extraordinary thing because he could make a kind of smile with his voice without smiling with his lips. His voice smiled while his face remained serious. It was a most forcible thing because it gave people the impression that he was being serious about being nice.

'Mesd'moiselles,' he said, and his voice was smiling. 'With the military there always has to be formality. It is something unavoidable. It is something that I regret exceedingly. But there can be chivalry also. And you must know that with the R.A.F. there is great chivalry. So now it will be a pleasure if you will all come in here and take with us a glass of beer. It is the chivalry of the military.' He stepped forward, opened the door of the café and said, 'Oh for God's sake, let's have a drink. Who wants a drink?'

Suddenly the girls saw it all. They saw the whole thing as it was, all of them at once. It took them by surprise. For a second they considered. Then they looked at one another, then they looked at the Stag, then they looked around at Stuffy and at William, and when they looked at those two they caught their eyes and the laughter that was in them. All at once the girls began to laugh and William laughed and Stuffy laughed and they moved forward and poured into the café.

The tall one with dark hair took the Stag by the arm and said, 'Mon Dieu, Military Police, mon Dieu, oh mon Dieu,' and she threw her head back and laughed and the Stag laughed with her. William said, 'It is the chivalry of the military,' and they moved into the café.

The place was rather like the one that they had been in before, wooden and sawdusty, and there were a few coffee-drinking Egyptians sitting around with the red tarbooshes on their heads. William and Stuffy pushed three round tables together and fetched chairs. The girls sat down. The Egyptians at the other tables put down their coffee cups, turned around in their chairs and gaped. They gaped like so many fat muddy fish, and some of them shifted their chairs round facing the party so that they could get a better view and they went on gaping.

A waiter came up and the Stag said, 'Seventeen beers. Bring us seventeen beers.' The waiter said 'Pleess' and went away.

As they sat waiting for the drinks the girls looked at the three pilots and the pilots looked at the girls. William said, 'It is the chivalry of the military,' and the tall dark girl said, 'Mon Dieu, you are crazy people, oh mon Dieu.'

The waiter brought the beer. William raised his glass and said, 'To the chivalry of the military.' The dark girl said, 'Oh mon Dieu.' Stuffy didn't say anything. He was busy looking around at the girls, sizing them up, trying to decide now which one he liked best so that he could go to work at once. The Stag was smiling and the girls were sitting there in their shiny evening dresses, shiny red, shiny gold, shiny blue, shiny green, shiny black and shiny silver, and once again it was almost a tableau, certainly it was a picture, and the girls were sitting there sipping their beer, seeming quite happy, not seeming suspicious any more because to them the whole thing now appeared exactly as it was and they understood.

'Jesus,' said the Stag. He put down his glass and looked

79

around him. 'Oh Jesus, there's enough here for the whole squadron. How I wish the whole squadron was here!' He took another drink, stopped in the middle of it and put down his glass quickly. 'I know what,' he said. 'Waiter, oh waiter.'

'Pleess.'

'Get me a big piece of paper and a pencil.'

'Pleess.' The waiter went away and came back with a sheet of paper. He took a pencil from behind his ear and handed it to the Stag. The Stag banged the table for silence.

'Mesd'moiselles,' he said, 'for the last time there is a formality. It is the last of all the formalities.'

'Of the military,' said William.

'Oh mon Dieu,' said the dark girl.

'It is nothing,' the Stag said. 'You are required to write your name and your telephone number on this piece of paper. It is for my friends in the squadron. It is so that they can be as happy as I am now, but without the same trouble beforehand.' The Stag's voice was smiling again. One could see that the girls liked his voice. 'You would be very kind if you would do that,' he went on, 'for they too would like to meet you. It would be a pleasure.'

'Wonderful,' said William.

'Crazy,' said the dark girl, but she wrote her name and number on the paper and passed it on. The Stag ordered another round of beer. The girls certainly looked funny sitting there in their dresses, but they were writing their names down on the paper. They looked happy and William particularly looked happy, but Stuffy looked serious because the problem of choosing was a weighty one and it was heavy on his mind. They were good-looking girls, young and good-looking, all different, completely different from each other because they were Greek and Syrian and French and Italian and light Egyptian and Yugoslav and many other things, but they were good-looking, all of them were good-looking and handsome.

The piece of paper had come back to the Stag now and they had all written on it; fourteen strangely written names and fourteen telephone numbers. The Stag looked at it slowly.

'This will go on the squadron notice-board,' he said, 'and I will be regarded as a great benefactor.'

William said, 'It should go to headquarters. It should be mimeographed and circulated to all squadrons. It would be good for morale.'

'Oh mon Dieu,' said the dark girl. 'You are crazy.'

Slowly Stuffy got to his feet, picked up his chair, carried it round to the other side of the table and pushed it between two of the girls. All he said was, 'Excuse me. Do you mind if I sit here?' At last he had made up his mind, and now he turned towards the one on his right and quietly went to work. She was very pretty; very dark and very pretty and she had plenty of shape. Stuffy began to talk to her, completely oblivious to the rest of the company, turning towards her and leaning his head on his hand. Watching him, it was not so difficult to understand why he was the greatest pilot in the squadron. He was a young concentrator, this Stuffy; an intense athletic concentrator who moved towards what he wanted in a dead straight line. He took hold of winding roads and carefully he made them straight, then he moved over them with great speed and nothing stopped him. He was like that, and now he was talking to the pretty girl but no one could hear what he was saying.

Meanwhile the Stag was thinking. He was thinking about the next move, and when everyone was getting towards the end of their third beer, he banged the table again for silence.

'Mesd'moiselles,' he said, 'It will be a pleasure for us to escort you home. I will take five of you,' – he had worked it all out – 'Stuffy will take five, and Jamface will take four. We will take three gharries and I will take five of you in mine and I will drop you home one at a time.'

William said, 'It is the chivalry of the military.'

'Stuffy,' said the Stag. 'Stuffy, is that all right? You take five. It's up to you whom you drop off last.'

Stuffy looked around. 'Yes,' he said. 'Oh yes. That suits me.'

'William, you take four. Drop them home one by one; you understand.'

'Perfectly,' said William. 'Oh perfectly.'

They all got up and moved towards the door. The tall one with dark hair took the Stag's arm and said, 'You take me?'

'Yes,' he answered. 'I take you.'

'You drop me off last?'

'Yes. I drop you off last.'

'Oh mon Dieu,' she said. 'That will be fine.'

Outside they got three gharries and they split up into parties. Stuffy was moving quickly. He got his girls into the carriage quickly, climbed in after them and the Stag saw the gharry drive off down the street. Then he saw William's gharry move off, but it seemed to start away with a sudden jerk, with the horses breaking into a gallop at once. The Stag looked again and he saw William perched high up on the driver's seat with the reins in his hands.

The Stag said, 'Let's go,' and his five girls got into their gharry. It was a squash, but everyone got in. The Stag sat back in his seat and then he felt an arm pushing up and under and linking with his. It was the tall one with dark hair. He turned and looked at her.

'Hello,' he said. 'Hello, you.'

'Ah,' she whispered. 'You are such goddam crazy people.' And the Stag felt a warmness inside him and he began to hum a little tune as the gharry rattled on through the dark streets.

Katina

Some brief notes about the last days of R.A.F.
fighters in the first Greek campaign.

Peter saw her first.

She was sitting on a stone, quite still, with her hands resting
on her lap. She was staring vacantly ahead, seeing nothing,
and all around, up and down the little street, people were running backward and forward with buckets of water, emptying
them through the windows of the burning houses.

Across the street on the cobblestones, there was a dead boy.
Someone had moved his body close in to the side so that it
would not be in the way.

A little farther down an old man was working on a pile of
stones and rubble. One by one he was carrying the stones away
and dumping them to the side. Sometimes he would bend
down and peer into the ruins, repeating a name over and over
again.

All around there was shouting and running and fires and
buckets of water and dust. And the girl sat quietly on the
stone, staring ahead, not moving. There was blood running
down the left side of her face. It ran down from her forehead
and dripped from her chin on to the dirty print dress she was
wearing.

Peter saw her and said, 'Look at that little girl.'

We went up to her and Fin put his hand on her shoulder,
bending down to examine the cut. 'Looks like a piece of shrap-
nel,' he said. 'She ought to see the Doc.'

Peter and I made a chair with our hands and Fin lifted her
up on to it. We started back through the streets and out towards the aerodrome, the two of us walking a little awk-
wardly, bending down, facing our burden. I could feel Peter's
fingers clasped tightly in mine and I could feel the buttocks of
the little girl resting lightly on my wrists. I was on the left side

and the blood was dripping down from her face on to the arm of my flying suit, running down the waterproof cloth on to the back of my hand. The girl never moved or said anything.

Fin said, 'She's bleeding rather fast. We'd better walk a bit quicker.'

I couldn't see much of her face because of the blood, but I could tell that she was lovely. She had high cheekbones and large round eyes, pale blue like an autumn sky, and her hair was short and fair. I guessed she was about nine years old.

This was in Greece in early April, 1941, at Paramythia. Our fighter squadron was stationed on a muddy field near the village. We were in a deep valley and all around us were the mountains. The freezing winter had passed, and now, almost before anyone knew it, spring had come. It had come quietly and swiftly, melting the ice on the lakes and brushing the snow off the mountain tops; and all over the airfield we could see the pale green shoots of grass pushing up through the mud, making a carpet for our landings. In our valley there were warm winds and wild flowers.

The Germans, who had pushed in through Yugoslavia a few days before, were now operating in force, and that afternoon they had come over very high with about thirty-five Dorniers and bombed the village. Peter and Fin and I were off duty for a while, and the three of us had gone down to see if there was anything we could do in the way of rescue work. We had spent a few hours digging around in the ruins and helping to put out fires, and we were on our way back when we saw the girl.

Now, as we approached the landing field, we could see the Hurricanes circling around coming in to land, and there was the Doc standing out in front of the dispersal tent, just as he should have been, waiting to see if anyone had been hurt. We walked towards him, carrying the child, and Fin, who was a few yards in front, said,

'Doc, you lazy old devil, here's a job for you.'

The Doc was young and kind and morose except when he got drunk. When he got drunk he sang very well.

'Take her into the sick bay,' he said. Peter and I carried her in and put her down on a chair. Then we left her and wandered over to the dispersal tent to see how the boys had got along.

It was beginning to get dark. There was a sunset behind the ridge over in the west, and there was a full moon, a bombers' moon, climbing up into the sky. The moon shone upon the shoulders of the tents and made them white; small white pyramids, standing up straight, clustering in little orderly groups around the edges of the aerodrome. They had a scared-sheep look about them the way they clustered themselves together, and they had a human look about them the way they stood up close to one another, and it seemed almost as though they knew that there was going to be trouble, as though someone had warned them that they might be forgotten and left behind. Even as I looked, I thought I saw them move. I thought I saw them huddle just a fraction nearer together.

And then, silently, without a sound, the mountains crept a little closer into our valley.

For the next two days there was much flying. There was the getting up at dawn, there was the flying, the fighting and the sleeping; and there was the retreat of the army. That was about all there was or all there was time for. But on the third day the clouds dropped down over the mountains and slid into the valley. And it rained. So we sat around in the mess-tent drinking beer and resinato, while the rain made a noise like a sewing machine on the roof. Then lunch. For the first time in days the whole squadron was present. Fifteen pilots at a long table with benches on either side and Monkey, the C.O. sitting at the head.

We were still in the middle of our fried corned beef when the flap of the tent opened and in came the Doc with an enormous dripping raincoat over his head. And with him, under the coat, was the little girl. She had a bandage round her head.

The Doc said, 'Hello. I've brought a guest.' We looked around and suddenly, automatically, we all stood up.

The Doc was taking off his raincoat and the little girl was standing there with her hands hanging loose by her sides looking at the men, and the men were all looking at her. With her fair hair and pale skin she looked less like a Greek than anyone I've ever seen. She was frightened by the fifteen scruffy-looking foreigners who had suddenly stood up when she came in, and for a moment she half-turned as if she were going to run away out into the rain.

Monkey said, 'Hallo. Hallo there. Come and sit down.'

'Talk Greek,' the Doc said. 'She doesn't understand.'

Fin and Peter and I looked at one another and Fin said, 'Good God, it's our little girl. Nice work, Doc.'

She recognized Fin and walked round to where he was standing. He took her by the hand and sat her down on the bench, and everyone else sat down too. We gave her some fried corned beef and she ate it slowly, looking down at her plate while she ate. Monkey said, 'Get Pericles.'

Pericles was the Greek interpreter attached to the squadron. He was a wonderful man we'd picked up at Yanina, where he had been the local school teacher. He had been out of work ever since the war started. 'The children do not come to school,' he said. 'They are up in the mountains and fight. I cannot teach sums to the stones.'

Pericles came in. He was old, with a beard, a long pointed nose and sad grey eyes. You couldn't see his mouth, but his beard had a way of smiling when he talked.

'Ask her her name,' said Monkey.

He said something to her in Greek. She looked up and said, 'Katina.' That was all she said.

'Look, Pericles,' Peter said, 'ask her what she was doing sitting by that heap of ruins in the village.'

Fin said, 'For God's sake leave her alone.'

'Ask her, Pericles,' said Peter.

'What should I ask?' said Pericles, frowning.

Peter said, 'What she was doing sitting on that heap of stuff in the village when we found her.'

Pericles sat down on the bench beside her and he talked to her again. He spoke gently and you could see that his beard was smiling a little as he spoke, helping her. She listened and it seemed a long time before she answered. When she spoke, it was only a few words, and the old man translated: 'She says that her family were under the stones.'

Outside the rain was coming down harder than ever. It beat upon the roof of the mess-tent so that the canvas shivered as the water bounced upon it. I got up and walked over and lifted the flap of the tent. The mountains were invisible behind the rain, but I knew they were around us on every side. I had a feeling that they were laughing at us, laughing at the smallness of our numbers and at the hopeless courage of the pilots. I felt that it was the mountains, not us, who were the clever ones. Had not the hills that very morning turned and looked northward towards Tepelene where they had seen a thousand German aircraft gathered under the shadow of Olympus? Was it not true that the snow on the top of Dodona had melted away in a day, sending little rivers of water running down across our landing field? Had not Kataphidi buried his head in a cloud so that our pilots might be tempted to fly through the whiteness and crash against his rugged shoulders?

And as I stood there looking at the rain through the tent flap, I knew for certain that the mountains had turned against us. I could feel it in my stomach.

I went back into the tent and there was Fin, sitting beside Katina, trying to teach her English words. I don't know whether he made much progress, but I do know that once he made her laugh and that was a wonderful thing for him to have done. I remember the sudden sound of her high laughter and how we all looked up and saw her face; how we saw how different it was to what it had been before. No one but Fin could have done it. He was so gay himself that it was difficult to be serious in his presence. He was gay and tall and black-haired, and he was sitting there on the bench, leaning forward, whispering and smiling, teaching Katina to speak English and teaching her how to laugh.

The next day the skies cleared and once again we saw the mountains. We did a patrol over the troops which were already retreating slowly towards Thermopylae, and we met some Messerschmitts and JU-87s dive-bombing the soldiers. I think we got a few of them, but they got Sandy. I saw him going down. I sat quite still for thirty seconds and watched his plane spiralling gently downward. I sat and waited for the parachute. I remember switching over my radio and saying quietly, 'Sandy, you must jump now. You must jump; you're getting near the ground.' But there was no parachute.

When we landed and taxied in, there was Katina, standing outside the dispersal tent with the Doc; a tiny shrimp of a girl in a dirty print dress, standing there watching the machines as they came in to land. To Fin, as he walked in, she said, 'Tha girisis xana.'

Fin said, 'What does it mean, Pericles?'

'It just means "you are back again",' and he smiled.

The child had counted the aircraft on her fingers as they took off, and now she noticed that there was one missing. We were standing around taking off our parachutes and she was trying to ask us about it, when suddenly someone said, 'Look out. Here they come.' They came through a gap in the hills, a mass of thin, black silhouettes, coming down upon the aerodrome.

There was a scramble for the slit trenches and I remember seeing Fin catch Katina round the waist and carry her off with us, and I remember seeing her fight like a tiger the whole way to the trenches.

As soon as we got into the trench and Fin had let her go, she jumped out and ran over on to the airfield. Down came the Messerschmitts with their guns blazing, swooping so low that you could see the noses of the pilots sticking out under their goggles. Their bullets threw up spurts of dust all around and I saw one of our Hurricanes burst into flames. I saw Katina standing right in the middle of the field, standing firmly with her legs astride and her back to us, looking up at the Germans as they dived past. I have never seen anything smaller and more angry and more fierce in my life. She seemed to be shouting at them, but the noise was great and one could hear nothing at all except the engines and the guns of the aeroplanes.

Then it was over. It was over as quickly as it had begun, and no one said very much except Fin, who said, 'I wouldn't have done that, ever; not even if I was crazy.'

That evening Monkey got out the squadron records and added Katina's name to the list of members, and the equipment officer was ordered to provide a tent for her. So, on the eleventh of April, 1941, she became a member of the squadron.

In two days she knew the first name or nickname of every pilot and Fin had already taught her to say 'Any luck?' and 'Nice work.'

But that was a time of much activity, and when I try to think of it hour by hour, the whole period becomes hazy in my mind. Mostly, I remember, it was escorting the Blenheims to Valona, and if it wasn't that, it was a ground-strafe of Italian trucks on the Albanian border or an S.O.S. from the Northumberland Regiment saying they were having the hell bombed out of them by half the aircraft in Europe.

None of that can I remember. I can remember nothing of that time clearly, save for two things. The one was Katina and how she was with us all the time; how she was everywhere and how wherever she went the people were pleased to see her. The other thing that I remember was when the Bull came into the mess-tent one evening after a lone patrol. The Bull was an enormous man with massive, slightly hunched shoulders and his chest was like the top of an oak table. Before the war he had done many things, most of them things which one could not do unless one conceded beforehand that there was no difference between life and death. He was quiet and casual and when he came into a room or into a tent, he always looked as though he had made a mistake and hadn't really meant to come in at all. It was getting dark and we were sitting round in the tent playing shove-halfpenny when the Bull came in. We knew that he had just landed.

He glanced around a little apologetically, then he said, 'Hello,' and wandered over to the bar and began to get out a bottle of beer.

Someone said, 'See anything, Bull?'

The Bull said, 'Yes,' and went on fiddling with the bottle of beer.

Katina

I suppose we were all very interested in our game of shove-halfpenny because no one said anything else for about five minutes. Then Peter said, 'What did you see, Bull?'

The Bull was leaning against the bar, alternately sipping his beer and trying to make a hooting noise by blowing down the neck of the empty bottle.

Peter said, 'What did you see?'

The Bull put down the bottle and looked up. 'Five S-79s,' he said.

I remember hearing him say it, but I remember also that our game was exciting and that Fin had one more shove to win. We all watched him miss it and Peter said, 'Fin, I think you're going to lose.' And Fin said, 'Go to hell.'

We finished the game, then I looked up and saw the Bull still leaning against the bar making noises with his beer bottle.

He said, 'This sounds like the old Mauretania coming into New York harbour,' and he started blowing into the bottle again.

'What happened with the S-79s?' I said.

He stopped his blowing and put down the bottle.

'I shot them down.'

Everyone heard it. At that moment eleven pilots in that tent stopped what they were doing and eleven heads flicked around and looked at the Bull. He took another drink of his beer and said quietly, 'At one time I counted eighteen parachutes in the air together.'

A few days later he went on patrol and did not come back.

Shortly afterwards Monkey got a message from Athens. It said that the squadron was to move down to Elevsis and from there do a defence of Athens itself and also cover the troops retreating through the Thermopylae Pass.

Katina was to go with the trucks and we told the Doc he was to see that she arrived safely. It would take them a day to make the journey. We flew over the mountains towards the south, fourteen of us, and at two-thirty we landed at Elevsis. It was a lovely aerodrome with runways and hangars; and best of all, Athens was only twenty-five minutes away by car.

That evening, as it was getting dark, I stood outside my tent. I stood with my hands in my pockets watching the sun go down and thinking of the work which we were to do. The more that I thought of it, the more impossible I knew it to be. I looked up, and once again I saw the mountains. They were closer to us here, crowding in upon us on all sides, standing shoulder to shoulder, tall and naked, with their heads in the clouds, surrounding us everywhere save in the south, where lay Piraeus and the open sea. I knew that each night, when it was very dark, when we were all tired and sleeping in our tents, those mountains would move forward, creeping a little closer, making no noise, until at last on the appointed day they would tumble forward with one great rush and push us into the sea.

Fin emerged from his tent.

'Have you seen the mountains?' I said.

'They're full of gods. They aren't any good,' he answered.

'I wish they'd stand still,' I said.

Fin looked up at the great crags of Parnes and Pentelikon.

'They're full of gods,' he said. 'Sometimes, in the middle of the night, when there is a moon, you can see the gods sitting on the summits. There was one on Kataphidi when we were at Paramythia. He was huge, like a house but without any shape and quite black.'

'You saw him?'

'Of course I saw him.'

'When?' I said. 'When did you see him, Fin?'

Fin said, 'Let's go into Athens. Let's go and look at the women in Athens.'

The next day the trucks carrying the ground staff and the equipment rumbled on to the aerodrome, and there was Katina sitting in the front seat of the leading vehicle with the Doc beside her. She waved to us as she jumped down, and she came running towards us, laughing and calling our names in a curious Greek way. She still had on the same dirty print dress and she still had a bandage round her forehead; but the sun was shining in her hair.

We showed her the tent which we had prepared for her and we showed her the small cotton nightdress which Fin had obtained in some mysterious way the night before in Athens. It was white with a lot of little blue birds embroidered on the front and we all thought that it was very beautiful. Katina wanted to put it on at once and it took a long time to persuade her that it was meant only for sleeping in. Six times Fin had to perform a complicated act which consisted of pretending to put on the nightdress, then jumping on to the bed and falling fast asleep. In the end she nodded vigorously and understood.

For the next two days nothing happened, except that the remnants of another squadron came down from the north and joined us. They brought six Hurricanes, so that altogether we had about twenty machines.

Then we waited.

On the third day German reconnaissance aircraft appeared, circling high over Piraeus, and we chased after them but never got up in time to catch them. This was understandable, because our radar was of a very special type. It is obsolete now, and I doubt whether it will ever be used again. All over the country, in all the villages, up on the mountains and out on the islands, there were Greeks, all of whom were connected to our small operations room by field telephone.

We had no operations officer, so we took it in turns to be on duty for the day. My turn came on the fourth day, and I remember clearly what happened.

At six-thirty in the morning the phone buzzed.

'This is A-7,' said a very Greek voice. 'This is A-7. There are noises overhead.'

I looked at the map. There was a little ring with 'A-7' written inside it just beside Yanina. I put a cross on the celluloid which covered the map and wrote 'Noises' beside it, as well as the time: '0631 hours.'

Three minutes later the phone went again.

'This is A-4. This is A-4. There are many noises above me,' said an old quavering voice, 'but I cannot see because there are thick clouds.'

I looked at the map. A-4 was Mt Karava. I made another cross on the celluloid and wrote 'Many noises – 0634,' and then I drew a line between Yanina and Karava. It pointed towards Athens, so I signalled the 'readiness' crew to scramble, and they took off and circled the city. Later they saw a Ju-88 on reconnaissance high above them, but they never caught it. It was in such a way that one worked the radar.

That evening when I came off duty I could not help thinking of the old Greek, sitting all alone in a hut up at A-4; sitting on the slope of Karava looking up into the whiteness and listening all day and all night for noises in the sky. I imagined the eagerness with which he seized the telephone when he heard something, and the joy he must have felt when the voice at the other end repeated his message and thanked him. I thought of his clothes and wondered if they were warm enough and I thought, for some reason, of his boots, which almost certainly had no soles left upon them and were stuffed with tree bark and paper.

That was April seventeenth. It was the evening when Monkey said, 'They say the Germans are at Lamia, which means that we're within range of their fighters. Tomorrow the fun should start.'

It did. At dawn the bombers came over, with the fighters circling around overhead, watching the bombers, waiting to pounce, but doing nothing unless someone interfered with the bombers.

I think we got eight Hurricanes into the air just before they arrived. It was not my turn to go up, so with Katina standing by my side I watched the battle from the ground. The child never said a word. Now and again she moved her head as she followed the little specks of silver dancing high above in the sky. I saw a plane coming down in a trail of black smoke and I looked at Katina. The hatred which was on the face of the child was the fierce burning hatred of an old woman who has hatred in her heart; it was an old woman's hatred and it was strange to see it.

In that battle we lost a sergeant called Donald.

At noon Monkey got another message from Athens. It said that morale was bad in the capital and that every available Hurricane was to fly in formation low over the city in order to show the inhabitants how strong we were and how many aircraft we had. Eighteen of us took off. We flew in tight formation up and down the main streets just above the roofs of the houses. I could see the people looking up, shielding their eyes from the sun, looking at us as we flew over, and in one street I saw an old woman who never looked up at all. None of them waved, and I knew then that they were resigned to their fate. None of them waved, and I knew, although I could not see their faces, that they were not even glad as we flew past.

Then we headed out towards Thermopylae, but on the way we circled the Acropolis twice. It was the first time I had seen it so close.

I saw a little hill – a mound almost, it seemed – and on the top of it I saw the white columns. There were a great number of them, grouped together in perfect order, not crowding one another, white in the sunshine, and I wondered, as I looked at them, how anyone could have put so much on top of so small a hill in such an elegant way.

Then we flew up the great Thermopylae Pass and I saw long lines of vehicles moving slowly southwards towards the sea. I saw occasional puffs of white smoke where a shell landed in the valley and I saw a direct hit on the road which made a gap in the line of trucks. But we saw no enemy aircraft.

When we landed Monkey said, 'Refuel quickly and get in the air again; I think they're waiting to catch us on the ground.'

But it was no use. They came down out of the sky five minutes after we had landed. I remember I was in the pilots' room in Number Two Hangar, talking to Fin and to a big tall man with rumpled hair called Paddy. We heard the bullets on the corrugated-iron roof of the hangar, then we heard explosions and the three of us dived under the little wooden table in the middle of the room. But the table upset. Paddy set it up again and crawled underneath. 'There's something about being under a table,' he said. 'I don't feel safe unless I'm under a table.'

Fin said, 'I never feel safe.' He was sitting on the floor watching the bullets making holes in the corrugated-iron wall of the room. There was a great clatter as the bullets hit the tin.

Then we became brave and got up and peeped outside the door. There were many Messerschmitt 109s circling the aerodrome, and one by one they straightened out and dived past the hangars, spraying the ground with their guns. But they did something else. They slid back their cockpit hoods and as they came past they threw out small bombs which exploded when they hit the ground and fiercely flung quantities of large lead balls in every direction. Those were the explosions which we had heard, and it was a great noise that the lead balls made as they hit the hangar.

Then I saw the men, the ground crews, standing up in their slit trenches firing at the Messerschmitts with rifles, reloading and firing as fast as they could, cursing and shouting as they shot, aiming ludicrously, hopelessly, aiming at an aeroplane with just a rifle. At Elevsis there were no other defences.

Suddenly the Messerschmitts all turned and headed for home, all except one, which glided down and made a smooth belly landing on the aerodrome.

Then there was chaos. The Greeks around us raised a shout and jumped on to the fire tender and headed out towards the crashed German aeroplane. At the same time more Greeks streamed out from every corner of the field, shouting and yelling and crying for the blood of the pilot. It was a mob intent upon vengeance and one could not blame them; but there were other considerations. We wanted the pilot for questioning, and we wanted him alive.

Monkey, who was standing on the tarmac, shouted to us, and Fin and Paddy and I raced with him towards the station wagon which was standing fifty yards away. Monkey was inside like a flash, started the engine and drove off just as the three of us jumped on the running board. The fire tender with the Greeks on it was not fast and it still had two hundred yards to go, and the other people had a long way to run. Monkey drove quickly and we beat them by about fifty yards.

We jumped up and ran over to the Messerschmitt, and there, sitting in the cockpit, was a fair-haired boy with pink cheeks and blue eyes. I have never seen anyone whose face showed so much fear.

Katina

He said to Monkey in English, 'I am hit in the leg.'

We pulled him out of the cockpit and got him into the car, while the Greeks stood around watching. The bullet had shattered the bone in his shin.

We drove him back and as we handed him over to the Doc, I saw Katina standing close, looking at the face of the German. This kid of nine was standing there looking at the German and she could not speak; she could not even move. She clutched the skirt of her dress in her hands and stared at the man's face. 'There is a mistake somewhere,' she seemed to be saying. 'There must be a mistake. This one has pink cheeks and fair hair and blue eyes. This cannot possibly be one of them. This is an ordinary boy.' She watched him as they put him on a stretcher and carried him off, then she turned and ran across the grass to her tent.

In the evening at supper I ate my fried sardines, but I could not eat the bread or the cheese. For three days I had been conscious of my stomach, of a hollow feeling such as one gets just before an operation or while waiting to have a tooth out in the dentist's house. I had had it all day for three days, from the moment I woke up to the time I fell asleep. Peter was sitting opposite me and I asked him about it.

'I've had it for a week,' he said. 'It's good for the bowels. It loosens them.'

'German aircraft are like liver pills,' said Fin from the bottom of the table. 'They are very good for you, aren't they, Doc?

The Doc said, 'Maybe you've had an overdose.'

'I have,' said Fin, 'I've had an overdose of German liver pills. I didn't read the instructions on the bottle. Take two before retiring.'

Peter said, 'I would love to retire.'

After supper three of us walked down to the hangars with Monkey, who said, 'I'm worried about this ground-strafing. They never attack the hangars because they know that we never put anything inside them. Tonight I think we'll collect four of the aircraft and put them into Number Two Hangar.'

That was a good idea. Normally the Hurricanes were dispersed all over the edge of the aerodrome, but they were being picked off one by one, because it was impossible to be in the air the whole time. The four of us took a machine each and taxied it into Number Two Hangar, and then we pulled the great sliding doors together and locked them.

The next morning, before the sun had risen from behind the mountains, a flock of JU-87s came over and blew Number Two Hangar right off the face of the earth. Their bombing was good and they did not even hit the hangars on either side of it.

That afternoon they got Peter. He went off towards a village called Khalkis, which was being bombed by JU-88s, and no one ever saw him again. Gay, laughing Peter, whose mother lived on a farm in Kent and who used to write to him in long, pale-blue envelopes which he carried about in his pockets.

I had always shared a tent with Peter, ever since I came to the squadron, and that evening after I had gone to bed he came back to that tent. You need not believe me; I do not expect you to, but I am telling you what happened.

I always went to bed first, because there is not room in one of those tents for two people to be turning around at the same time. Peter usually came in two or three minutes afterwards. That evening I went to bed and I lày thinking that tonight he would not be coming. I wondered whether his body lay tangled in the wreckage of his aircraft on the side of some bleak mountain or whether it was at the bottom of the sea, and I hoped only that he had had a decent funeral.

Suddenly I heard a movement. The flap of the tent opened and it shut again. But there were no footsteps. Then I heard him sit down on his bed. It was a noise that I had heard every night for weeks past and always it had been the same. It was just a thump and a creaking of the wooden legs of the camp bed. One after the other the flying boots were pulled off and dropped upon the ground, and as always one of them took three times as long to get off as the other. After that there was the gentle rustle of a blanket being pulled back and then the creakings of the rickety bed as it took the weight of a man's body.

They were sounds I had heard every night, the same sounds

in the same order, and now I sat up in bed and said, 'Peter.' It was dark in the tent. My voice sounded very loud.

'Hallo, Peter. That was tough luck you had today.' But there was no answer.

I did not feel uneasy or frightened, but I remember at the time touching the tip of my nose with my finger to make sure that I was there; then because I was very tired, I went to sleep.

In the morning I looked at the bed and saw it had been slept in. But I did not show it to anyone, not even to Fin. I put the blankets back in place myself and patted the pillow.

It was on that day, the twentieth of April, 1941, that we fought the Battle of Athens. It was perhaps the last of the great dog-fighting air battles that will ever be fought, because nowadays the planes fly always in great formations of wings and squadrons, and attack is carried out methodically and scientifically upon the orders of the leader. Nowadays one does not dog-fight at all over the sky except upon very rare occasions. But the Battle of Athens was a long and beautiful dog-fight in which fifteen Hurricanes fought for half an hour with between one hundred and fifty and two hundred German bombers and fighters.

The bombers started coming over early in the afternoon. It was a lovely spring day and for the first time the sun had in it a trace of real summer warmth. The sky was blue, save for a few wispy clouds here and there and the mountains stood out black and clear against the blue of the sky.

Pentelikon no longer hid his head in the clouds. He stood over us, grim and forbidding, watching every move and knowing that each thing we did was of little purpose. Men were foolish and were made only so that they should die, while mountains and rivers went on for ever and did not notice the passing of time. Had not Pentelikon himself many years ago looked down upon Thermopylae and seen a handful of Spartans defending the pass against the invaders; seen them fight until there was not one man left alive among them? Had he not seen the Persians cut to pieces by Leonidas at Marathon, and had he not looked down upon Salamis and upon the sea when Themistocles and the Athenians drove the enemy from their shores, causing them to lose more than two hundred sail? All these things and many more he had seen, and now he looked down upon us, we were as nothing in his eyes. Almost there was a look of scorn upon the face of the mountain, and I thought for a moment that I could hear the laughter of the gods. They knew so well that we were not enough and that in the end we must lose.

The bombers came over just after lunch, and at once we saw that there were a great number of them. We looked up and saw that the sky was full of little silver specks and the sunlight danced and sparkled upon a hundred different pairs of wings.

There were fifteen Hurricanes in all and they fought like a storm in the sky. It is not easy to remember much about such a battle, but I remember looking up and seeing in the sky a mass of small black dots. I remember thinking to myself that those could not be aeroplanes; they simply could not be aeroplanes, because there were not so many aeroplanes in the world.

Then they were on us, and I remember that I applied a little flap so that I should be able to turn in tighter circles; then I remember only one or two small incidents which photographed themselves upon my mind. There were the spurts of flame from the guns of a Messerschmitt as he attacked from the frontal quarter of my starboard side. There was the German whose parachute was on fire as it opened. There was the German who flew up beside me and made rude signs at me with his fingers. There was the Hurricane which collided with a Messerschmitt. There was the aeroplane which collided with a man who was descending in a parachute, and which went into a crazy frightful spin towards the earth with the man and the parachute dangling from its port wing. There were the two bombers which collided while swerving to avoid a fighter, and I remember distinctly seeing a man being thrown clear out of the smoke and debris of the collision, hanging in mid-air with his arms outstretched and his legs apart. I tell you there was nothing that did not happen in that battle. There was the moment when I saw a single Hurricane doing tight turns around the summit of Mt Parnes with nine Messerschmitts on its tail and then I remember that suddenly the skies seemed to clear. There were no longer any aircraft in sight. The battle was over. I turned around and headed back towards Elevsis, and as I went I looked down and saw Athens and Piraeus and the rim of the sea as it curved around the gulf and travelled southward towards the Mediterranean. I saw the port of Piraeus where the bombs had fallen and I saw the smoke and fire rising above the docks. I saw the narrow coastal plain, and on it I saw tiny bonfires, thin columns of black smoke curling upward and drifting away to the east. They were the fires of aircraft which had been shot down, and I hoped only that none of them were Hurricanes.

Just then I ran straight into a Junkers 88; a straggler, the last bomber returning from the raid. He was in trouble and there was black smoke streaming from one of his engines. Although I shot at him, I don't think that it made any difference. He was coming down anyway. We were over the sea and I could tell that he wouldn't make the land. He didn't. He came down smoothly on his belly in the blue Gulf of Piraeus, two miles from the shore. I followed him and circled, waiting to make sure that the crew got out safely into their dinghy.

Slowly the machine began to sink, dipping its nose under the water and lifting its tail into the air. But there was no sign of the crew. Suddenly, without any warning, the rear gun started to fire. They opened up with their rear gun and the bullets made small jagged holes in my starboard wing. I swerved away and I remember shouting at them. I slid back the hood of the cockpit and shouted, 'You lousy brave bastards. I hope you drown.' The bomber sank soon backwards.

When I got back they were all standing around outside the hangars counting the score, and Katina was sitting on a box with tears rolling down her cheeks. But she was not crying, and Fin was kneeling down beside her, talking to her in English, quietly and gently, forgetting that she could not understand.

We lost one third of our Hurricanes in that battle, but the Germans lost more.

The Doc was dressing someone who had been burnt and he

looked up and said, 'You should have heard the Greeks on the aerodrome cheering as the bombers fell out of the sky.'

As we stood around talking, a truck drove up and a Greek got out and said that he had some pieces of body inside. 'This is the watch,' he said, 'that was on the arm.' It was a silver wrist watch with a luminous dial, and on the back there were some initials. We did not look inside the truck.

Now we had, I think, nine Hurricanes left.

That evening a very senior R.A.F. officer came out from Athens and said, 'Tomorrow at dawn you will all fly to Megara. It is about ten miles down the coast. There is a small field there on which you can land. The Army is working on it throughout the night. They have two big rollers there and they are rolling it smooth. The moment you land you must hide your aircraft in the olive grove which is on the south side of the field. The ground staff are going farther south to Argos and you can join them later, but you may be able to operate from Megara for a day or two.'

Fin said, 'Where's Katina? Doc, you must find Katina and see that she gets to Argos safely.'

The Doc said, 'I will,' and we knew that we could trust him.

At dawn the next morning, when it was still dark, we took off and flew to the little field at Megara, ten miles away. We landed and hid our Hurricanes in the olive grove and broke off branches of the trees and put them over the aircraft. Then we sat down on the slope of a small hill and waited for orders.

As the sun rose up over the mountains we looked across the field and saw a mass of Greek villagers coming down from the village of Megara, coming down towards our field. There were many hundreds of them, women and children mostly, and they all came down towards our field, hurrying as they came.

Fin said, 'What the hell,' and we sat up on our little hill and watched, wondering what they were going to do.

They dispersed all around the edge of the field and gathered armfuls of heather and bracken. They carried it out on to the field, and forming themselves into long lines, they began to scatter the heather and the bracken over the grass. They were camouflaging our landing field. The rollers, when they had rolled out the ground and made it flat for landing, had left marks which were easily visible from above, and so the Greeks came out of their village, every man, woman and child, and began to put matters right. To this day I do not know who told them to do it. They stretched in a long line across the field, walking forward slowly and scattering the heather, and Fin and I went out and walked among them.

They were old women and old men mostly, very small and very sad-looking, with dark, deeply wrinkled faces and they worked slowly scattering the heather. As we walked by, they would stop their work and smile, saying something in Greek which we could not understand. One of the children gave Fin a small pink flower and he did not know what to do with it, but walked around carrying it in his hand.

Then we went back to the slope of the hill and waited. Soon the field telephone buzzed. It was the very senior officer speaking. He said that someone must fly back to Elevsis at once and collect important messages and money. He said also that all of us must leave our little field at Megara and go to Argos that evening. The others said that they would wait until I came back with the money so that we could all fly to Argos together.

At the same time, someone had told the two Army men who were still rolling our field, to destroy their rollers so that the Germans would not get them. I remember, as I was getting into my Hurricane, seeing the two huge rollers charging towards each other across the field and I remember seeing the Army men jump aside just before they collided. There was a great crash and I saw all the Greeks who were scattering heather stop in their work and look up. For a moment they stood rock still, looking at the rollers. Then one of them started to run. It was an old woman and she started to run back to the village as fast as she could, shouting something as she went, and instantly every man, woman and child in the field seemed to take fright and ran after her. I wanted to get out and run beside them and explain to them; to say I was sorry but that there was nothing else we could do. I wanted to tell them that we would not forget them and that one day we would come back. But it was no use. Bewildered and frightened, they ran back to their homes, and they did not stop running until they were out of sight, not even the old men.

I took off and flew to Elevsis. I landed on a dead aerodrome. There was not a soul to be seen. I parked my Hurricane, and as I walked over to the hangars the bombers came over once again. I hid in a ditch until they had finished their work, then got up and walked over to the small operations room. The telephone was still on the table, so for some reason I picked up the receiver and said, 'Hallo.'

A rather German voice at the other end answered.

I said, 'Can you hear me?' and the voice said:

'Yes, yes, I can hear you.'

'All right,' I said, 'listen carefully.'

'Yes, continue please.'

'This is the R.A.F. speaking. And one day we will come back, do you understand. One day we will come back.'

Then I tore the telephone from its socket and threw it through the glass of the closed window. When I went outside there was a small man in civilian clothes standing near the door. He had a revolver in one hand and a small bag in the other.

'Do you want anything?' he said in quite good English.

I said, 'Yes, I want important messages and papers which I am to carry back to Argos.'

'Here you are,' he said, as he handed me the bag. 'And good luck.'

I flew back to Megara. There were two Greek destroyers standing offshore, burning and sinking. I circled our field and the others taxied out, took off and we all flew off towards Argos.

The landing ground at Argos was just a kind of small field. It was surrounded by thick olive groves into which we taxied our aircraft for hiding. I don't know how long the field was, but it was not easy to land upon it. You had to come in low hanging on the prop, and the moment you touched down you had to start putting on brake, jerking it on and jerking it off again the moment she started to nose over. But only one man overshot and crashed.

The ground staff had arrived already and as we got out of our aircraft Katina came running up with a basket of black olives, offering them to us and pointing to our stomachs, indicating that we must eat.

Fin bent down and ruffled her hair with his hand. He said, 'Katina, one day we must go into town and buy you a new dress.' She smiled at him but did not understand and we all started to eat black olives.

Then I looked around and saw that the wood was full of aircraft. Around every corner there was an aeroplane hidden in the trees, and when we asked about it we learned that the Greeks had brought the whole of their air force down to Argos and parked them in that little wood. They were peculiar ancient models, not one of them less than five years old, and I don't know how many dozen there were there.

That night we slept under the trees. We wrapped Katina up in a large flying suit and gave her a flying helmet for a pillow, and after she had gone to sleep we sat around eating black olives and drinking resinato out of an enormous cask. But we were very tired, and soon we fell asleep.

All the next day we saw the truckloads of troops moving down the road towards the sea, and as often as we could we took off and flew above them.

The Germans kept coming over and bombing the road near by, but they had not yet spotted our airfield.

Later in the day we were told that every available Hurricane was to take off at six p.m. to protect an important shipping move, and the nine machines, which were all that were now left, were refuelled and got ready. At three minutes to six we began to taxi out of the olive grove on to the field.

The first two machines took off, but just as they left the ground something black swept down out of the sky and shot them both down in flames. I looked around and saw at least fifty Messerschmitt 110s circling our field, and even as I looked some of them turned and came down upon the remaining seven Hurricanes which were waiting to take off.

There was no time to do anything. Each one of our aircraft was hit in that first swoop, although funnily enough only one of the pilots was hurt. It was impossible now to take off, so we jumped out of our aircraft, hauled the wounded pilot out of his cockpit and ran with him back to the slit trenches, to the wonderful big, deep zig-zagging slit trenches which had been dug by the Greeks.

The Messerschmitts took their time. There was no opposition either from the ground or from the air, except that Fin was firing his revolver.

It is not a pleasant thing to be ground-strafed especially if they have cannon in their wings; and unless one has a deep slit trench in which to lie, there is no future in it. For some reason, perhaps because they thought it was a good joke, the German pilots went for the slit trenches before they bothered about the aircraft. The first ten minutes was spent rushing madly around the corners of the trenches so as not to be caught in a trench which ran parallel with the line of flight of the attacking aircraft. It was a hectic, dreadful ten minutes, with everyone shouting 'Here comes another,' and scrambling and rushing to get around the corner into the other section of the trench.

Then the Germans went for the Hurricanes and at the same time for the mass of old Greek aircraft parked all around the olive grove, and one by one, methodically and systematically, they set them on fire. The noise was terrific, and everywhere – in the trees, on the rocks and on the grass – the bullets splattered.

I remember peeping cautiously over the top of our trench and seeing a small white flower growing just a few inches away from my nose. It was pure white and it had three petals. I remember looking past it and seeing three of the Germans diving on my own Hurricane which was parked on the other side of the field and I remember shouting at them, although I do not know what I said.

Then suddenly I saw Katina. She was running out from the far corner of the aerodrome, running right out into the middle of this mass of blazing guns and burning aircraft, running as fast as she could. Once she stumbled, but she scrambled to her feet again and went on running. Then she stopped and stood looking up, raising her fists at the planes as they flew past.

Now as she stood there, I remember seeing one of the Messerschmitts turning and coming in low straight towards her and I remember thinking that she was so small that she could not be hit. I remember seeing the spurts of flame from his guns as he came, and I remember seeing the child, for a split second, standing quite still, facing the machine. I remember that the wind was blowing in her hair.

Then she was down.

The next moment I shall never forget. On every side, as if by magic, men appeared out of the ground. They swarmed out of their trenches and like a crazy mob poured on to the aerodrome, running towards the tiny little bundle which lay motionless in the middle of the field. They ran fast, crouching as they went, and I remember jumping up out of my slit trench and joining with them. I remember thinking of nothing at all and watching the boots of the man in front of me, noticing that he was a little bow-legged and that his blue trousers were much too long.

I remember seeing Fin arrive first, followed closely by a sergeant called Wishful, and I remember seeing the two of them pick up Katina and start running with her back towards the trenches. I saw her leg, which was just a lot of blood and bones, and I saw her chest where the blood was spurting out on to her white print dress; I saw, for a moment, her face, which was white as the snow on top of Olympus.

I ran beside Fin, and as he ran, he kept saying, 'The lousy bastards, the lousy, bloody bastards'; and then as we got to our trench I remember looking round and finding that there was no longer any noise or shooting. The Germans had gone.

Fin said, 'Where's the Doc?' and suddenly there he was, standing beside us, looking at Katina – looking at her face.

The Doc gently touched her wrist and without looking up he said, 'She is not alive.'

They put her down under a little tree, and when I turned away I saw on all sides the fires of countless burning aircraft. I saw my own Hurricane burning near by and I stood staring hopelessly into the flames as they danced around the engine and licked against the metal of the wings.

I stood staring into the flames, and as I stared, the fire became a deeper red and I saw beyond it not a tangled mass of smoking wreckage, but the flames of a hotter and intenser fire which now burned and smouldered in the hearts of the people of Greece.

Still I stared, and as I stared I saw in the centre of the fire, whence the red flames sprang, a bright, white heat, shining bright and without any colour.

As I stared, the brightness diffused and became soft and yellow like sunlight, and through it, beyond it, I saw a young child standing in the middle of a field with the sunlight shining in her hair. For a moment she stood looking up into the sky, which was clear and blue and without any clouds; then she turned and looked towards me, and as she turned I saw that the front of her white print dress was stained deep red, the colour of blood.

Then there was no longer any fire or any flames and I saw before me only the glowing twisted wreckage of a burned-out plane. I must have been standing there for quite a long time.

Yesterday was Beautiful

He bent down and rubbed his ankle where it had been sprained with the walking so that he couldn't see the ankle bone. Then he straightened up and looked around him. He felt in his pocket for a packet of cigarettes, took one out and lit it. He wiped the sweat from his forehead with the back of his hand and he stood in the middle of the street looking around him.

'Dammit, there must be someone here,' he said aloud, and he felt better when he heard the sound of his voice.

He walked on, limping, walking on the toe of his injured foot, and when he turned the next corner he saw the sea and the way the road curved around between the ruined houses and went on down the hill to the edge of the water. The sea was calm and black. He could clearly make out the line of hills on the mainland in the distance and he estimated that it was about eight miles away. He bent down again to rub his ankle. 'God dammit,' he said. 'There must be some of them still alive.' But there was no noise anywhere, and there was a stillness about the buildings and about the whole village which made it seem as though the place had been dead for a thousand years.

Suddenly he heard a little noise as though someone had moved his feet on the gravel and when he looked around he saw the old man. He was sitting in the shade on a stone beside a water trough, and it seemed strange that he hadn't seen him before.

'Health to you,' said the pilot. 'Ghia sou.'

He had learned Greek from the people up around Larissa and Yanina.

The old man looked up slowly, turning his head but not moving his shoulders. He had a greyish-white beard. He had a cloth cap on his head and he wore a shirt which had no collar.

It was a grey shirt with thin black stripes. He looked at the pilot and he was like a blind man who looks towards something but does not see.

'Old man, I am glad to see you. Are there no other people in the village?'

There was no answer.

The pilot sat down on the edge of the water trough to rest his ankle.

'I am Inglese,' he said. 'I am an aviator who has been shot down and jumped out by the parachute. I am Inglese.'

The old man moved his head slowly up and down. 'Inglesus,' he said quietly. 'You are Inglesus.'

'Yes, I am looking for someone who has a boat. I wish to go back to the mainland.

There was a pause, and when he spoke, the old man seemed to be talking in his sleep. 'They come over all the time,' he said. 'The Germanoi they come over all the time.' The voice had no expression. He looked up into the sky, then he turned and looked behind him in the sky. 'They will come again today, Inglese. They will come again soon.' There was no anxiety in his voice. There was no expression whatsoever. 'I do not understand why they come to us,' he added.

The pilot said, 'Perhaps not today. It is late now. I think they have finished for today.'

'I do not understand why they come to us, Inglese. There is no one here.'

The pilot said, 'I am looking for a man who has a boat who can take me across to the mainland. Is there a boat owner now in the village?'

'A boat?'

'Yes.' There was a pause while the question was considered. 'There is such a man.'

'Could I find him? Where does he live?'

'There is a man in the village who owns a boat.'

'Please tell me what is his name?'

The old man looked up again at the sky. 'Joannis is the one here who has a boat.'

'Joannis who?'

'Joannis Spirakis,' and he smiled. The name seemed to have a significance for the old man and he smiled.

'Where does he live?' the pilot said. 'I am sorry to be giving you this trouble.'

'Where he lives?'

'Yes.'

The old man considered this too. Then he turned and looked down the street towards the sea. 'Joannis was living in the house nearest to the water. But his house isn't any more. The Germanoi hit it this morning. It was early and it was still dark. You can see the house isn't any more. It isn't any more.'

'Where is he now?'

'He is living in the house of Antonina Angelou. That house there with the red colour on the window.' He pointed down the street.

'Thank you very much. I will go and call on the boat owner.'

'Ever since he was a boy,' the old man went on, 'Joannis has had a boat. His boat is white with a blue line around the top,' and he smiled again. 'But at the moment I do not think he will be in the house. His wife will be there. Anna wil' be there, with Antonina Angelou. They will be home.'

'Thank you again. I will go and speak to his wife.'

The pilot got up and started to go down the street, but almost at once the man called after him, 'Inglese.'

The pilot turned.

'When you speak to the wife of Joannis – when you speak to Anna ... you should remember something.' He paused, searching for words. His voice wasn't expressionless any longer and he was looking up at the pilot.

'Her daughter was in the house when the Germanoi came. It is just something that you should remember.'

The pilot stood on the road waiting.

'Maria. Her name was Maria.'

'I will remember,' answered the pilot. 'I am sorry.'

He turned away and walked down the hill to the house with the red windows. He knocked and waited. He knocked again louder and waited. There was the noise of footsteps and the door opened.

It was dark in the house and all he could see was that the woman had black hair and that her eyes were black like her hair. She looked at the pilot who was standing out in the sunshine.

'Health to you,' he said. 'I am Inglese.'

She did not move.

'I am looking for Joannis Spirakis. They say that he owns a boat.'

Still she did not move.

'Is he in the house?'

'No.'

'Perhaps his wife is here. She could know where he is.'

At first there was no answer. Then the woman stepped back and held open the door. 'Come in, Inglesus,' she said.

He followed her down the passage and into a back room. The room was dark because there was no glass in the windows – only patches of cardboard. But he could see the old woman who was sitting on the bench with her arms resting on the table. She was tiny. She was small like a child and her face was like a little screwed-up ball of brown paper.

'Who is it?' she said in a high voice.

The first woman said, 'This is an Inglesus. He is looking for your husband because he requires a boat.'

'Health to you, Inglesus,' the old woman said.

The pilot stood by the door, just inside the room. The first woman stood by the window and her arms hung down by her sides.

The old woman said, 'Where are the Germanoi?' Her voice seemed bigger than her body.

'Now they are around Lamia.'

'Lamia.' She nodded. 'Soon they will be here. Perhaps tomorrow they will be here. But I do not care. Do you hear me, Inglesus, I do not care.' She was leaning forward a little in her chair and the pitch of her voice was becoming higher. 'When they come it will be nothing new. They have already been here. Every day they have been here. Every day they come over and they bom bom bom and you shut your eyes and you open them again and you get up and you go outside and the houses are just dust – and the people.' Her voice rose and fell.

She paused, breathing quickly, then she spoke more quietly. 'How many have you killed, Inglesus?'

The pilot put out a hand and leaned against the door to rest his ankle.

'I have killed some,' he said quietly.

'How many?'

'As many as I could, old woman. We cannot count the number of men.'

'Kill them all,' she said softly. 'Go and kill every man and every woman and every baby. Do you hear me, Inglesus? You must kill them all.' The little brown ball of paper became smaller and more screwed up. 'The first one I see I shall kill.' She paused. 'And then, Inglesus, and then later, his family will hear that he is dead.'

The pilot did not say anything. She looked up at him and her voice was different. 'What is it you want Inglesus?'

He said, 'About the Germanoi, I am sorry. But there is not much we can do.'

'No,' she answered, 'there is nothing. And you?'

'I am looking for Joannis. I wish to use his boat.'

'Joannis,' she said quietly, 'he is not here. He is out.'

Suddenly she pushed back the bench, got to her feet and went out of the room. 'Come,' she said. He followed her down the passage towards the front door. She looked even smaller when she was standing than when she was sitting down and she walked quickly down the passage towards the door and opened it. She stepped out into the sunshine and for the first time he saw how very old she was.

She had no lips. Her mouth was just wrinkled skin like the rest of her face and she screwed up her eyes at the sun and looked up the road.

'There he is,' she said. 'That's him.' She pointed at the old man who was sitting beside the drinking trough.

The pilot looked at the man. Then he turned to speak to the old woman, but she had disappeared into the house.

They Shall Not Grow Old

The two of us sat outside the hangar on wooden boxes.

It was noon. The sun was high and the heat of the sun was like a close fire. It was hotter than hell out there by the hangar. We could feel the hot air touching the inside of our lungs when we breathed and we found it better if we almost closed our lips and breathed in quickly; it was cooler that way. The sun was upon our shoulders and upon our backs, and all the time the sweat seeped out from our skin, trickled down our necks, over our chests and down our stomachs. It collected just where our belts were tight around the tops of our trousers and it filtered under the tightness of our belts where the wet was very uncomfortable and made prickly heat on the skin.

Our two Hurricanes were standing a few yards away, each with that patient, smug look which fighter planes have when the engine is not turning, and beyond them the thin black strip of the runway sloped down towards the beaches and towards the sea. The black surface of the runway and the white grassy sand on the sides of the runway shimmered and shimmered in the sun. The heat haze hung like a vapour over the aerodrome.

The Stag looked at his watch.

'He ought to be back,' he said.

The two of us were on readiness, sitting there for orders to take off. The Stag moved his feet on the hot ground.

'He ought to be back,' he said.

It was two and a half hours since Fin had gone and he certainly should have come back by now. I looked up into the sky and listened. There was the noise of airmen talking beside the petrol wagon and there was the faint pounding of the sea upon the beaches; but there was no sign of an aeroplane. We sat a little while longer without speaking.

'It looks as though he's had it,' I said.

'Yep,' said the Stag. 'It looks like it.'

The Stag got up and put his hands into the pockets of his khaki shorts. I got up too. We stood looking northwards into the clear sky, and we shifted our feet on the ground because of the softness of the tar and because of the heat.

'What was the name of that girl?' said the Stag without turning his head.

'Nikki,' I answered.

The Stag sat down again on his wooden box, still with his hands in his pockets and he looked down at the ground between his feet. The Stag was the oldest pilot in the squadron; he was twenty-seven. He had a mass of coarse ginger hair which he never brushed. His face was pale, even after all this time in the sun, and covered with freckles. His mouth was wide and tight closed. He was not tall but his shoulders under his khaki shirt were broad and thick like those of a wrestler. He was a quiet person.

'He'll probably be all right,' he said, looking up. 'And anyway, I'd like to meet the Vichy Frenchman who can get Fin.'

We were in Palestine fighting the Vichy French in Syria. We were at Haifa, and three hours before the Stag, Fin and I had gone on readiness. Fin had flown off in response to an urgent call from the Navy, who had phoned up and said that there were two French destroyers moving out of Beyrouth harbour. Please go at once and see where they are going, said the Navy. Just fly up the coast and have a look and come back quickly and tell us where they are going.

So Fin had flown off in his Hurricane. The time had gone by and he had not returned. We knew that there was no longer much hope. If he hadn't been shot down, he would have run out of petrol some time ago.

I looked down and I saw his blue R.A.F. cap which was lying on the ground where he had thrown it as he ran to his aircraft, and I saw the oil stains on top of the cap and the shabby bent peak. It was difficult now to believe that he had gone. He had been in Egypt, in Libya and in Greece. On the aerodrome and in the mess we had had him with us all of the time. He was gay and tall and full of laughter, this Fin, with black hair and a long straight nose which he used to stroke up and down with the tip of his finger. He had a way of listening to you while you were telling a story, leaning back in his chair with his face to the ceiling but with his eyes looking down on the ground, and it was only last night at supper that he had suddenly said, 'You know, I wouldn't mind marrying Nikki. I think she's a good girl.'

The Stag was sitting opposite him at the time, eating baked beans.

'You mean just occasionally,' he said.

Nikki was in a cabaret in Haifa.

'No,' said Fin. 'Cabaret girls make fine wives. They are never unfaithful. There is no novelty for them in being unfaithful; that would be like going back to the old job.'

The Stag had looked up from his beans. 'Don't be such a bloody fool,' he said. 'You wouldn't really marry Nikki.'

'Nikki,' said Fin with great seriousness, 'comes of a fine family. She is a good girl. She never uses a pillow when she sleeps. Do you know why she never uses a pillow when she sleeps?'

'No.'

The others at the table were listening now. Everyone was listening to Fin talking about Nikki.

'Well, when she was very young she was engaged to be married to an officer in the French Navy. She loved him greatly. Then one day when they were sunbathing together on the beach he happened to mention to her that he never used a pillow when he slept. It was just one of those little things which people say to each other for the sake of conversation. But Nikki never forgot it. From that time onwards she began to practise sleeping without a pillow. One day the French officer was run over by a truck and killed; but although to her it was very uncomfortable, she still went on sleeping without a pillow to preserve the memory of her lover.'

Fin took a mouthful of beans and chewed them slowly. 'It is a sad story,' he said. 'It shows that she is a good girl. I think I would like to marry her.'

That was what Fin had said last night at supper. Now he was gone and I wondered what little thing Nikki would do in his memory.

The sun was hot on my back and I turned instinctively in order to take the heat upon the other side of my body. As I turned, I saw Carmel and the town of Haifa. I saw the steep pale-green slope of the mountain as it dropped down towards the sea, and below it I saw the town and the bright colours of the houses shining in the sun. The houses with their white-washed walls covered the sides of Carmel and the red roofs of the houses were like a rash on the face of the mountain.

Walking slowly towards us from the grey corrugated iron hangar, came the three men who were the next crew on readiness. They had their yellow Mae Wests slung over their shoulders and they came walking slowly towards us, holding their helmets in their hands as they came.

When they were close, the Stag said, 'Fin's had it,' and they said, 'Yes, we know.' They sat down on the wooden boxes which we had been using, and immediately the sun was upon their shoulders and upon their backs and they began to sweat. The Stag and I walked away.

The next day was a Sunday and in the morning we flew up the Lebanon valley to ground-strafe an aerodrome called Rayak. We flew past Hermon who had a hat of snow upon his head, and we came down out of the sun on to Rayak and on to the French bombers on the aerodrome and began our strafing. I remember that as we flew past, skimming low over the ground, the doors of the French bombers opened. I remember seeing a whole lot of women in white dresses running out across the aerodrome; I remember particularly their white dresses.

You see, it was a Sunday and the French pilots had asked their ladies out from Beyrouth to look over the bombers. The Vichy pilots had said, come out on Sunday morning and we will show you our aeroplanes. It was a very Vichy French thing for them to do.

So when we started shooting, they all tumbled out and began to run across the aerodrome in their white Sunday dresses.

I remember hearing Monkey's voice over the radio, saying, 'Give them a chance, give them a chance,' and the whole squadron wheeled around and circled the aerodrome once while the women ran over the grass in every direction. One of them stumbled and fell twice and one of them was limping and being helped by a man, but we gave them time. I remember watching the small bright flashes of a machine gun on the ground and thinking that they should at least have stopped their shooting while we were waiting for their white-dressed women to get out of the way.

That was the day after Fin had gone. The next day the Stag and I sat once more at readiness on the wooden boxes outside the hangar. Paddy, a big fair-haired boy, had taken Fin's place and was sitting with us.

It was noon. The sun was high and the heat of the sun was like a close fire. The sweat ran down our necks, down inside our shirts, over our chests and stomachs, and we sat there waiting for the time when we would be relieved. The Stag was sewing the strap on to his helmet with a needle and cotton and telling of how he had seen Nikki the night before in Haifa and of how he had told her about Fin.

Suddenly we heard the noise of an aeroplane. The Stag stopped his talking and we all looked up. The noise was coming from the north, and it grew louder and louder as the aeroplane flew closer, and then the Stag said suddenly, 'It's a Hurricane.'

The next moment it was circling the aerodrome, lowering its wheels to land.

'Who is it?' said the fair-haired Paddy. 'No one's gone out this morning.'

Then, as it glided past us on to the runway, we saw the number on the tail of the machine, H.4427, and we knew that it was Fin.

We were standing up now, watching the machine as it taxied towards us, and when it came up close and swung round for parking we saw Fin in the cockpit. He waved his hand at us, grinned and got out. We ran up and shouted at him, 'Where've you been?' 'Where in the hell have you been?'

'Did you force-land and get away again?' 'Did you find a woman in Beyrouth?' 'Fin, where in the hell have you been?'

Others were coming up and crowding around him now, fitters and riggers and the men who drove the fire tender, and they all waited to hear what Fin would say. He stood there pulling off his helmet, pushing back his black hair with his hand, and he was so astonished at our behaviour that at first he merely looked at us and did not speak. Then he laughed and he said, 'What in the hell's the matter? What's the matter with all of you?'

'Where have you been?' we shouted. 'Where have you been for two days?'

Upon the face of Fin there was a great and enormous astonishment. He looked quickly at his watch.

'Five past twelve,' he said. 'I left at eleven, one hour and five minutes ago. Don't be a lot of damn fools. I must go and report quickly. The Navy will want to know that those destroyers are still in the harbour at Beyrouth.'

He started to walk away; I caught his arm.

'Fin,' I said quietly, 'you've been away since the day before yesterday. What's the matter with you?'

He looked at me and laughed.

'I've seen you organize much better jokes than this one,' he said. 'It isn't so funny. It isn't a bit funny.' And he walked away.

We stood there, the Stag, Paddy and I, the fitters, the riggers and the men who drove the fire-engine, watching Fin as he walked away. We looked at each other, not knowing what to say or to think, understanding nothing, knowing nothing except that Fin had been serious when he spoke and that what he said he had believed to be true. We knew this because we knew Fin, and we knew it because when one has been together as we had been together, then there is never any doubting of anything that anyone says when he is talking about his flying: there can only be a doubting of one's self. These men were doubting themselves, standing there in the sun doubting themselves, and the Stag was standing by the wing of Fin's machine peeling off with his fingers little flakes of paint which had dried up and cracked in the sun.

Someone said, 'Well, I'll be buggered,' and the men turned and started to walk quietly back to their jobs. The next three pilots on readiness came walking slowly towards us from the grey corrugated-iron hangar, walking slowly under the heat of the sun and swinging their helmets in their hands as they came. The Stag, Paddy and I walked over to the pilots' mess to have a drink and lunch.

The mess was a small white wooden building with a verandah. Inside there were two rooms, one a sitting room with armchairs and magazines and a hole in the wall through which you could buy drinks, and the other a dining room with one long wooden table. In the sitting room we found Fin talking to Monkey, our C.O. The other pilots were sitting around listening and everybody was drinking beer. We knew that it was really a serious business in spite of the beer and the armchairs; that Monkey was doing what he had to do and doing it in the only way possible. Monkey was a rare man, tall with a handsome face, an Italian bullet wound in his leg and a casual friendly efficiency. He never laughed out loud, he just choked and grunted deep in his throat.

Fin was saying, 'You must go easy, Monkey; you must help me to stop thinking that I've gone mad.'

Fin was being serious and sensible, but he was worried as hell.

'I have told you all I know,' he said. 'That I took off at eleven o'clock, that I climbed up high, that I flew to Beyrouth, saw the two French destroyers and came back, landing at five past twelve. I swear to you that that is all I know.'

He looked around at us, at the Stag and me, at Paddy and Johnny and the half-dozen other pilots in the room, and we smiled at him and nodded to show him that we were with him, not against him, and that we believed what he said.

Monkey said, 'What in the hell am I going to say to Headquarters at Jerusalem? I reported you missing. Now I've got to report your return. They'll insist on knowing where you've been.'

The whole thing was getting to be too much for Fin. He was sitting upright, tapping with the fingers of his left hand on the leather arm of his chair, tapping with quick sharp taps, leaning forward, thinking, thinking, fighting to think, tapping on the arm of the chair and then he began tapping the floor with his foot as well. The Stag could stand it no longer.

'Monkey,' he said, 'Monkey, let's just leave it all for a bit. Let's leave it and perhaps Fin will remember something later on.'

Paddy, who was sitting on the arm of the Stag's chair, said, 'Yes, and meanwhile we could tell H.Q. that Fin had force-landed in a field in Syria, taken two days to repair his aircraft, then flown home.'

Everybody was helping Fin. The pilots were all helping him. In the mind of each of us was the certain knowledge that here was something that concerned us greatly. Fin knew it, although that was all he knew, and the others knew it because one could see it upon their faces. There was a tension, a fine high-drawn tension in the room, because here for the first time was something which was neither bullets nor fire nor the coughing of an engine nor burst tyres nor blood in the cockpit nor yesterday nor today, nor even tomorrow. Monkey felt it too, and he said, 'Yes, let's have another drink and leave it for a bit. I'll tell H.Q. that you force-landed in Syria and managed to get off again later.'

We had some more beer and went in to lunch. Monkey ordered bottles of Palestine white wine with the meal to celebrate Fin's return.

After that no one mentioned the thing at all; we did not even talk about it when Fin wasn't there. But each one of us continued to think about it secretly, knowing for certain that it was something important and that it was not finished. The tension spread quickly through the squadron and it was with all the pilots.

Meanwhile the days went by and the sun shone upon the aerodrome and upon the aircraft and Fin took his place among us flying in the normal way.

Then one day, I think it was about a week later, we did

another ground-strafe of Rayak aerodrome. There were six of us, with Monkey leading and Fin flying on his starboard side. We came in low over Rayak and there was plenty of light flak, and as we went in on the first run, Paddy's machine was hit. As we wheeled for the second run we saw his Hurricane wing gently over and dive straight to the ground at the edge of the aerodrome. There was a great billow of white smoke as it hit, then the flames, and as the flames spread the smoke turned from white to black and Paddy was with it. Immediately there was a crackle over the radio and I heard Fin's voice, very excited, shouting into his microphone, shouting, 'I've remembered it. Hello, Monkey, I've remembered it all,' and Monkey's calm slow reply, 'O.K. Fin, O.K.; don't forget it.'

We did our second run and then Monkey led us quickly away, weaving in and out of the valleys, with the bare grey brown hills far above us on either side, and all the way home, all through the half-hour's flight, Fin never stopped shouting over the R.T. First he would call to Monkey and say, 'Hello, Monkey, I've remembered it, all of it; every bit of it.' Then he would say, 'Hello, Stag, I've remembered it, all of it; I can't forget it now.' He called me and he called Johnny and he called Wishful; he called us all separately over and over again, and he was so excited that sometimes he shouted too loudly into his mike and we could not hear what he was saying.

When we landed, we dispersed our aircraft and because Fin for some reason had to park his at the far side of the aerodrome, the rest of us were in the Operations room before him.

The Ops room was beside the hangar. It was a bare place with a large table in the middle of the floor on which there was a map of the area. There was another smaller table with a couple of telephones, a few wooden chairs and benches and at one end the floor was stacked with Mae Wests, parachutes and helmets. We were standing there taking off our flying clothing and throwing it on to the floor at the end of the room when Fin arrived. He came quickly into the doorway and stopped. His black hair was standing up straight and untidy because of the way in which he had pulled off his helmet; his face was shiny with sweat and his khaki shirt was dark and wet. His mouth was open and he was breathing quickly. He looked as though he had been running. He looked like a child who had rushed downstairs into a room full of grown-ups to say that the cat has had kittens in the nursery and who does not know how to begin.

We had all heard him coming because that was what we had been waiting for. Everyone stopped what they were doing and stood still, looking at Fin.

Monkey said, 'Hello Fin,' and Fin said, 'Monkey, you've got to believe this because it's what happened.'

Monkey was standing over by the table with the telephones; the Stag was near him, square short ginger-haired Stag, standing up straight, holding a Mae West in his hand, looking at Fin. The others were at the far end of the room. When Fin spoke, they began to move up quietly until they were closer to him, until they reached the edge of the big map table which they touched with their hands. There they stood, looking at Fin, waiting for him to begin.

He started at once, talking quickly, then calming down and talking more slowly as he got into his story. He told everything, standing there by the door of the Ops room, with his yellow Mae West still on him and with his helmet and oxygen mask in his hand. The others stayed where they were and listened, and as I listened to him, I forgot that it was Fin speaking and that we were in the Ops room at Haifa; I forgot everything and went with him on his journey, and did not come back until he had finished.

'I was flying at about twenty thousand,' he said. 'I flew over Tyre and Sidon and over the Damour River and then I flew inland over the Lebanon hills, because I intended to approach Beyrouth from the east. Suddenly I flew into cloud, thick white cloud which was so thick and dense that I could see nothing except the inside of my cockpit. I couldn't understand it, because a moment before everything had been clear and blue and there had been no cloud anywhere.

'I started to lose height to get out of the cloud and I went down and down and still I was in it. I knew that I must not go too low because of the hills, but at six thousand the cloud was still around me. It was so thick that I could see nothing, not even the nose of my machine nor the wings, and the cloud condensed on the windshield and little rivers of water ran down the glass and got blown away by the slipstream. I have never seen cloud like that before. It was thick and white right up to the edges of the cockpit. I felt like a man on a magic carpet, sitting there alone in this little glass-topped cockpit, with no wings, no tail, no engine and no aeroplane.

'I knew that I must get out of this cloud, so I turned and flew west over the sea away from the mountains; then I came down low by my altimeter. I came down to five hundred feet, four hundred, three hundred, two hundred, one hundred, and the cloud was still around me. For a moment I paused. I knew that it was unsafe to go lower. Then, quite suddenly, like a gust of wind, came the feeling that there was nothing below me; no sea nor earth nor anything else and slowly, deliberately, I opened the throttle, pushed the stick hard forward and dived.

'I did not watch the altimeter; I looked straight ahead through the windshield at the whiteness of the cloud and I went on diving. I sat there pressing the stick forward, keeping her in the dive, watching the vast clinging whiteness of the cloud and I never once wondered where I was going. I just went.

'I do not know how long I sat there; it may have been minutes and it may have been hours; I know only that as I sat there and kept her diving, I was certain that what was below me was neither mountains nor rivers nor earth nor sea and I was not afraid.

'Then I was blinded. It was like being half asleep in bed when someone turns on the light.

'I came out of the cloud so suddenly and so quickly that I was blinded. There was no space of time between being in it and being out of it. One moment I was in it and the whiteness was thick around me and in that same moment I was out of it and the light was so bright that I was blinded. I screwed up my eyes and held them tight closed for several seconds.

'When I opened them everything was blue, more blue than anything that I had ever seen. It was not a dark blue, nor was it a bright blue; it was a blue blue, a pure shining colour which I had never seen before and which I cannot describe. I looked around. I looked up above me and behind me. I sat up and peered below me through the glass of the cockpit and everywhere it was blue. It was bright and clear, like pleasant sunlight, but there was no sun.

'Then I saw them.

'Far ahead and above I saw a long thin line of aircraft flying across the sky. They were moving forward in a single black line, all at the same speed, all in the same direction, all close up, following one behind the other, and the line stretched across the sky as far as the eye could see. It was the way they moved ahead, the urgent way in which they pressed forward forward forward like ships sailing before a great wind, it was from this that I knew everything. I do not know why or how I knew it, but I knew as I looked at them that these were the pilots and air crews who had been killed in battle, who now, in their own aircraft were making their last flight, their last journey.

'As I flew higher and closer I could recognize the machines themselves. I saw in that long procession nearly every type there was. I saw Lancasters and Dorniers, Halifaxes and Hurricanes, Messerschmitts, Spitfires, Stirlings, Savoia 79s, Junker 88s, Gladiators, Hampdens, Macchi 200s, Blenheims, Focke Wulfs, Beaufighters, Swordfish and Heinkels. All these and many more I saw, and the moving line reached across the blue sky both to the one side and to the other until it faded from sight.

'I was close to them now and I began to sense that I was being sucked towards them regardless of what I wished to do. There was a wind which took hold of my machine, blew it over and tossed it about like a leaf and I was pulled and sucked as by a giant vortex towards the other aeroplanes. There was nothing I could do for I was in the vortex and in the arms of the wind. This all happened very quickly, but I remember it clearly. I felt the pull on my aircraft becoming stronger; I was whisked forward faster and faster, and then suddenly I was flying in the procession itself, moving forward with the others, at the same speed and on the same course. Ahead of me, close enough for me to see the colour of the paint on its wings, was a Swordfish, an old Fleet Air Arm Swordfish. I could see the heads and helmets of the observer and the pilot as they sat in their cockpits, the one behind the other. Ahead of the Swordfish there was a Dornier, a Flying Pencil, and beyond the Dornier there were others which I could not recognize from where I was.

'We flew on and on. I could not have turned and flown away even if I had wanted to. I do not know why, although it may have been something to do with the vortex and with the wind, but I knew that it was so. Moreover, I was not really flying my aircraft; it flew itself. There was no manoeuvring to reckon with, no speed, no height, no throttle, no stick, no nothing. Once I glanced down at my instruments and saw that they were all dead, just as they are when the machine is sitting on the ground.

'So we flew on. I had no idea how fast we went. There was no sensation of speed and for all I know, it was a million miles an hour. Now I come to think of it, I never once during that time, felt either hot or cold or hungry or thirsty; I felt none of those things. I felt no fear, because I knew nothing of which to be afraid. I felt no worry, because I could remember nothing or think of nothing about which to be worried. I felt no desire to do anything that I was not doing or to have anything that I did not have, because there was nothing that I wished to do and there was nothing that I wished to have. I felt only pleasure at being where I was, at seeing the wonderful light and the beautiful colour around me. Once I caught sight of my face in the cockpit mirror and I saw that I was smiling, smiling with my eyes and with my mouth, and when I looked away I knew that I was still smiling, simply because that was the way I felt. Once, the observer in the Swordfish ahead of me turned and waved his hand. I slid back the roof of my cockpit and waved back. I remember that even when I opened the cockpit, there was no rush of air and no rush of cold or heat, nor was there any pressure of the slipstream on my hand. Then I noticed that they were all waving at each other, like children on a roller-coaster and I turned and waved at the man in the Macchi behind me.

'But there was something happening along the line. Far up in front I could see that the aeroplanes had changed course, were wheeling around to the left and losing height. The whole procession, as it reached a certain point, was banking around and gliding downwards in a wide, sweeping circle. Instinctively I glanced down over the cockpit, and there I saw spread out below me a vast green plain. It was green and smooth and beautiful; it reached to the far edges of the horizon where the blue of the sky came down and merged with the green of the plain.

'And there was the light. Over to the left, far away in the distance was a bright white light, shining bright and without any colour. It was as though the sun, but something far bigger than the sun, something without shape or form whose light was bright but not blinding, was lying on the far edge of the green plain. The light spread outwards from a centre of brilliance and it spread far up into the sky and far out over the plain. When I saw it, I could not at first look away from it. I had no desire to go towards it, into it, and almost at once the desire and the longing became so intense that several times I tried to pull my aircraft out of the line and fly straight towards it; but it was not possible and I had to fly with the rest.

'As they banked around and lost height I went with them, and we began to glide down towards the green plain below. Now that I was closer, I could see the great mass of aircraft upon the plain itself. They were everywhere, scattered over the ground like currants upon a green carpet. There were hundreds and hundreds of them, and each minute, each second almost, their numbers grew as those in front of me landed and taxied to a standstill.

'Quickly we lost height. Soon I saw that the ones just in front of me were lowering their wheels and preparing to land. The Dornier next but one to me levelled off and touched down. Then the old Swordfish. The pilot turned a little to the left out of the way of the Dornier and landed beside him. I turned to the left of the Swordfish and levelled off. I looked out of the cockpit at the ground, judging the height, and I saw the green of the ground blurred as it rushed past me and below me.

'I waited for my aircraft to sink and to touch down. It seemed to take a long time. "Come on," I said. "Come on, come on." I was only about six feet up, but she would not sink. "Get down," I shouted, "please *get down*." I began to panic. I became frightened. Suddenly I noticed that I was gaining speed. I cut all the switches but it made no difference. The aircraft was gathering speed, going faster and faster, and I looked around and saw behind me the long procession of aircraft dropping down out of the sky and sweeping in to land. I saw the mass of machines upon the ground, scattered far across the plain and away on one side I saw the light, that shining white light which shone so brightly over the great plain and to which I longed to go. I know that had I been able to land, I would have started to run towards that light the moment I got out of my aircraft.

'And now I was flying away from it. My fear grew. As I flew faster and farther away, the fear took hold of me until soon I was fighting crazy mad, pulling at the stick, wrestling with the aeroplane, trying to turn it around, back towards the light. When I saw that it was impossible, I tried to kill myself. I really wanted to kill myself then. I tried to dive the aircraft into the ground, but it flew on straight. I tried to jump out of the cockpit, but there was a hand upon my shoulder which held me down. I tried to bang my head against the sides of the cockpit, but it made no difference and I sat there fighting with my machine and with everything until suddenly I noticed that I was in cloud. I was in the same thick white cloud as before; and I seemed to be climbing. I looked behind me, but the cloud had closed in all round. There was nothing now but this vast impenetrable whiteness. I began to feel sick and giddy. I did not care any longer what happened one way or the other, I just sat there limply, letting the machine fly on by itself.

'It seemed a long time and I am sure that I sat there for many hours. I must have gone to sleep. As I slept, I dreamed. I dreamed not of the things that I had just seen, but of the things of my ordinary life, of the squadron, of Nikki and of the aerodrome here at Haifa. I dreamed that I was sitting at readiness outside the hangar with two others, that a request came from the Navy for someone to do a quick recco over Beyrouth; and because I was first up, I jumped into my Hurricane and went off. I dreamed that I passed over Tyre and Sidon and over the Damour River, climbing up to twenty thousand as I went. Then I turned inland over the Lebanon hills, swung around and approached Beyrouth from the east. I was above the town, peering over the side of the cockpit, looking for the harbour and trying to find the two French destroyers. Soon I saw them, saw them clearly, tied up close alongside each other by the wharf, and I banked around and dived for home as fast as I could.

'The Navy's wrong, I thought to myself as I flew back. The destroyers are still in the harbour. I looked at my watch. An hour and a half. "I've been quick," I said. "They'll be pleased." I tried to call up on the radio to give the information, but I couldn't get through.

'Then I came back here. When I landed, you all crowded around me and asked me where I had been for two days, but I could remember nothing. I did not remember anything except the flight to Beyrouth until just now, when I saw Paddy being shot down. As his machine hit the ground, I found myself saying, "You lucky bastard. You lucky, lucky bastard," and as I said it, I knew why I was saying it and remembered everything. That was when I shouted to you over the radio. That was when I remembered.'

Fin had finished. No one had moved or said anything all the time that he had been talking. Now it was only Monkey who spoke. He shuffled his feet on the floor, turned and looked out of the window and said quietly, almost in a whisper, 'Well, I'll be damned,' and the rest of us went slowly back to the business of taking off our flying clothing and stacking it in the corner of the room on the floor; all except the Stag, square short Stag, who stood there watching Fin as Fin walked slowly across the room to put away his clothing.

After Fin's story, the squadron returned to normal. The tension which had been with us for over a week, disappeared. The aerodrome was a happier place in which to be. But no one ever mentioned Fin's journey. We never once spoke about it together, not even when we got drunk in the evening at the Excelsior in Haifa.

The Syrian campaign was coming to an end. Everyone could see that it must finish soon, although the Vichy people were still fighting fiercely south of Beyrouth. We were still flying. We were flying a great deal over the fleet, which was bombarding the coast, for we had the job of protecting them from the Junker 88s which came over from Rhodes. It was on the last one of these flights over the fleet that Fin was killed.

We were flying high above the ships when the Ju-88s came over in force and there was a battle. We had only six Hurricanes in the air; there were many of the Junkers and it was a good fight. I do not remember much about what went on at the time. One never does. But I remember that it was a hectic, chasing fight, with the Junkers diving for the ships, with the ships barking at them, throwing up everything into the air so that the sky was full of white flowers which blossomed quickly and grew and blew away with the wind. I remember the German who blew up in mid-air, quickly, with just a white flash, so that where the bomber had been, there was nothing left except tiny little pieces falling slowly downwards. I remember the one that had its rear turret shot away, which flew along with the gunner hanging out of the tail by his straps, struggling to get back into the machine. I remember one, a brave one who stayed up above to fight us while the others went down to dive-bomb. I remember that we shot him up and I remember seeing him turn slowly over on to his back, pale green belly upwards like a dead fish, before finally he spun down.

And I remember Fin.

I was close to him when his aircraft caught fire. I could see the flames coming out of the nose of his machine and dancing over the engine cowling. There was black smoke coming from the exhaust of his Hurricane.

I flew up close and I called to him over the R.T. 'Hello, Fin,' I called, 'you'd better jump.'

His voice came back, calm and slow. 'It's not so easy.'

'Jump,' I shouted, 'jump quickly.'

I could see him sitting there under the glass roof of the cockpit. He looked towards me and shook his head.

'It's not so easy,' he answered. 'I'm a bit shot up. My arms are shot up and I can't undo the straps.'

'Get out,' I shouted. 'For God's sake, get out,' but he did not answer. For a moment his aircraft flew on, straight and level, then gently, like a dying eagle, it dipped a wing and dived towards the sea. I watched it as it went; I watched the thin trail of black smoke which it made across the sky, and as I watched, Fin's voice came again over the radio, clear and slow. 'I'm a lucky bastard,' he was saying. 'A lucky, lucky bastard.'

Beware of the Dog

Down below there was only a vast white undulating sea of cloud. Above there was the sun, and the sun was white like the clouds, because it is never yellow when one looks at it from high in the air.

He was still flying the Spitfire. His right hand was on the stick and he was working the rudder-bar with his left leg alone. It was quite easy. The machine was flying well. He knew what he was doing.

Everything is fine, he thought. I'm doing all right. I'm doing nicely. I know my way home. I'll be there in half an hour. When I land I shall taxi in and switch off my engine and I shall say, help me to get out, will you. I shall make my voice sound ordinary and natural and none of them will take any notice. Then I shall say, someone help me to get out. I can't do it alone because I've lost one of my legs. They'll all laugh and think that I'm joking and I shall say, all right, come and have a look, you unbelieving bastards. Then Yorky will climb up on to the wing and look inside. He'll probably be sick because of all the blood and the mess. I shall laugh and say, for God's sake, help me get out.

He glanced down again at his right leg. There was not much of it left. The cannon-shell had taken him on the thigh, just above the knee, and now there was nothing but a great mess and a lot of blood. But there was no pain. When he looked down, he felt as though he were seeing something that did not belong to him. It had nothing to do with him. It was just a mess which happened to be there in the cockpit; something strange and unusual and rather interesting. It was like finding a dead cat on the sofa.

He really felt fine, and because he still felt fine, he felt excited and unafraid.

I won't even bother to call up on the radio for the blood-wagon, he thought. It isn't necessary. And when I land I'll sit there quite normally and say, some of you fellows come and help me out, will you, because I've lost one of my legs. That will be funny. I'll laugh a little while I'm saying it; I'll say it calmly and slowly, and they'll think I'm joking. When Yorky comes up on to the wing and gets sick, I'll say, Yorky you old son of a bitch, have you fixed my car yet. Then when I get out I'll make my report. Later I'll go up to London. I'll take that half bottle of whisky with me and I'll give it to Bluey. We'll sit in her room and drink it. I'll get the water out of the bathroom tap. I won't say much until it's time to go to bed, then I'll say, Bluey I've got a surprise for you. I lost a leg today. But I don't mind so long as you don't. It doesn't even hurt. We'll go everywhere in cars. I always hated walking except when I walked down the street of the coppersmiths in Baghdad, but I could go in a rickshaw. I could go home and chop wood, but the head always flies off the axe. Hot water, that's what it needs; put it in the bath and make the handle swell. I chopped lots of wood last time I went home and I put the axe in the bath ...

Then he saw the sun shining on the engine cowling of his machine. He saw the sun shining on the rivets in the metal, and he remembered the aeroplane and he remembered where he was. He realized that he was no longer feeling good; that he was sick and giddy. His head kept falling forward on to his chest because his neck seemed no longer to have any strength. But he knew that he was flying the Spitfire. He could feel the handle of the stick between the fingers of his right hand.

I'm going to pass out, he thought. Any moment now I'm going to pass out.

He looked at his altimeter. Twenty-one thousand. To test himself he tried to read the hundreds as well as the thousands. Twenty-one thousand and what? As he looked the dial became blurred and he could not even see the needle. He knew then that he must bale out; that there was not a second to lose, otherwise he would become unconscious. Quickly, frantically, he tried to slide back the hood with his left hand, but he had not the strength. For a second he took his right hand off the stick and with both hands he managed to push the hood back. The rush of cold air on his face seemed to help. He had a moment of great clearness. His actions became orderly and precise. That is what happens with a good pilot. He took some quick deep breaths from his oxygen mask, and as he did so, he looked out over the side of the cockpit. Down below there was only a vast white sea of cloud and he realized that he did not know where he was.

It'll be the Channel, he thought. I'm sure to fall in the drink.

He throttled back, pulled off his helmet, undid his straps and pushed the stick hard over to the left. The Spitfire dipped its port wing and turned smoothly over on to its back. The pilot fell out.

As he fell, he opened his eyes, because he knew that he must not pass out before he had pulled the cord. On one side he saw the sun; on the other he saw the whiteness of the clouds, and as he fell, as he somersaulted in the air, the white clouds chased the sun and the sun chased the clouds. They chased each other in a small circle; they ran faster and faster and there was the sun and the clouds and the clouds and the sun, and the clouds came nearer until suddenly there was no longer any sun but only a great whiteness. The whole world was white and there was nothing in it. It was so white that sometimes it looked black, and after a time it was either white or black, but mostly it was white. He watched it as it turned from white to black, then back to white again, and the white stayed for a long time, but the black lasted only for a few seconds. He got into the habit of going to sleep during the white periods, of waking up just in time to see the world when it was black. The black was very quick. Sometimes it was only a flash, a flash of black lightning. The white was slow and in the slowness of it, he always dozed off.

One day, when it was white, he put out a hand and he touched something. He took it between his fingers and crumpled it. For a time he lay there, idly letting the tips of his fingers play with the thing which they had touched. Then slowly he opened his eyes, looked down at his hand and saw that he was holding something which was white. It was the edge of a sheet. He knew it was a sheet because he could see the texture of the material and the stitchings on the hem. He screwed up his eyes and opened them again quickly. This time he saw the room. He saw the bed in which he was lying: he saw the grey walls and the door and the green curtains over the window. There were some roses on the table by his bed.

Then he saw the basin on the table near the roses. It was a white enamel basin and beside it there was a small medicine glass.

This is a hospital, he thought. I am in a hospital. But he could remember nothing. He lay back on his pillow, looking at the ceiling and wondering what had happened. He was gazing at the smooth greyness of the ceiling which was so clean and grey, and then suddenly he saw a fly walking upon it. The sight of this fly, the suddenness of seeing this small black speck on a sea of grey, brushed the surface of his brain, and quickly, in that second, he remembered everything. He remembered the Spitfire and he remembered the altimeter showing twenty-one thousand feet. He remembered the pushing back of the hood with both hands and he remembered the baling out. He remembered his leg.

It seemed all right now. He looked down at the end of the bed, but he could not tell. He put one hand underneath the bedclothes and felt for his knees. He found one of them, but when he felt for the other, his hand touched something which was soft and covered in bandages.

Just then the door opened and a nurse came in.

'Hello,' she said. 'So you've waked up at last.'

She was not good-looking, but she was large and clean. She was between thirty and forty and she had fair hair. More than that he did not notice.

'Where am I?'

'You're a lucky fellow. You landed in a wood near the beach. You're in Brighton. They brought you in two days ago, and now you're all fixed up. You look fine.'

'I've lost a leg,' he said.

'That's nothing. We'll get you another one. Now you must go to sleep. The doctor will be coming to see you in about an hour.' She picked up the basin and the medicine glass and went out.

But he did not sleep. He wanted to keep his eyes open because he was frightened that if he shut them again everything would go away. He lay looking at the ceiling. The fly was still there. It was very energetic. It would run forward very fast for a few inches, then it would stop. Then it would run forward again, stop, run forward, and every now and then it would take off and buzz around viciously in small circles. It always landed back in the same place on the ceiling and started running and stopping all over again. He watched it for so long that after a while it was no longer a fly, but only a black speck upon a sea of grey, and he was still watching it when the nurse opened the door, and stood aside while the doctor came in. He was an Army doctor, a major, and he had some last war ribbons on his chest. He was bald and small, but he had a cheerful face and kind eyes.

'Well, well,' he said. 'So you've decided to wake up at last. How are you feeling?'

'I feel all right.'

'That's the stuff. You'll be up and about in no time.'

The doctor took his wrist to feel his pulse.

'By the way,' he said, 'some of the lads from your squadron were ringing up and asking about you. They wanted to come along and see you, but I said that they'd better wait a day or two. Told them you were all right and that they could come and see you a little later on. Just lie quiet and take it easy for a bit. Got something to read?' He glanced at the table with the roses. 'No. Well, nurse will look after you. She'll get you anything you want.' With that he waved his hand and went out, followed by the large clean nurse.

When they had gone, he lay back and looked at the ceiling again. The fly was still there and as he lay watching it he heard the noise of an aeroplane in the distance. He lay listening to the sound of its engines. It was a long way away. I wonder what it is, he thought. Let me see if I can place it. Suddenly he jerked his head sharply to one side. Anyone who has been bombed can tell the noise of a Junkers 88. They can tell most other German bombers for that matter, but especially a Junkers 88. The engines seem to sing a duet. There is a deep vibrating bass voice and with it there is a high pitched tenor. It is the singing of the tenor which makes the sound of a Ju-88 something which one cannot mistake.

He lay listening to the noise and he felt quite certain about what it was. But where were the sirens and where the guns? That German pilot certainly had a nerve coming near Brighton alone in daylight.

The aircraft was always far away and soon the noise faded away into the distance. Later on there was another. This one, too, was far away, but there was the same deep undulating bass and the high swinging tenor and there was no mistaking it. He had heard that noise every day during the Battle.

He was puzzled. There was a bell on the table by the bed. He reached out his hand and rang it. He heard the noise of footsteps down the corridor. The nurse came in.

'Nurse, what were those aeroplanes?'

'I'm sure I don't know. I didn't hear them. Probably fighters or bombers. I expect they were returning from France. Why, what's the matter?'

'They were Ju-88s. I'm sure they were Ju-88s. I know the sound of the engines. There were two of them. What were they doing over here?'

The nurse came up to the side of his bed and began to straighten out the sheets and tuck them in under the mattress.

'Gracious me, what things you imagine. You mustn't worry about a thing like that. Would you like me to get you something to read?'

'No, thank you.'

She patted his pillow and brushed back the hair from his forehead with her hand.

'They never come over in daylight any longer. You know that. They were probably Lancasters or Flying Fortresses.'

'Nurse.'

'Yes.'

'Could I have a cigarette?'

'Why certainly you can.'

She went out and came back almost at once with a packet of Players and some matches. She handed one to him and when he had put it in his mouth, she struck a match and lit it.

'If you want me again,' she said, 'just ring the bell,' and she went out.

Once towards evening he heard the noise of another aircraft. It was far away, but even so he knew that it was a single-engined machine. It was going fast; he could tell that. He could not place it. It wasn't a Spit, and it wasn't a Hurricane. It did not sound like an American engine either. They make more noise. He did not know what it was, and it worried him greatly. Perhaps I am very ill, he thought. Perhaps I am imagining things. Perhaps I am a little delirious. I simply do not know what to think.

That evening the nurse came in with a basin of hot water and began to wash him.

'Well,' she said, 'I hope you don't think that we're being bombed.'

She had taken off his pyjama top and was soaping his right arm with a flannel. He did not answer.

She rinsed the flannel in the water, rubbed more soap on it, and began to wash his chest.

'You're looking fine this evening,' she said. 'They operated on you as soon as you came in. They did a marvellous job. You'll be all right. I've got a brother in the R.A.F.,' she added. 'Flying bombers.'

He said, 'I went to school in Brighton.'

She looked up quickly. 'Well, that's fine,' she said. 'I expect you'll know some people in the town.'

'Yes,' he said, 'I know quite a few.'

She had finished washing his chest and arms. Now she turned back the bedclothes so that his left leg was uncovered. She did it in such a way that his bandaged stump remained under the sheets. She undid the cord of his pyjama trousers and took them off. There was no trouble because they had cut off the right trouser leg so that it could not interfere with the bandages. She began to wash his left leg and the rest of his body. This was the first time he had had a bed-bath and he was embarrassed. She laid a towel under his leg and began washing his foot with the flannel. She said, 'This wretched soap won't lather at all. It's the water. It's as hard as nails.'

He said, 'None of the soap is very good now and, of course, with hard water it's hopeless.' As he said it he remembered something. He remembered the baths which he used to take at school in Brighton, in the long stone-floored bathroom which had four baths in a row. He remembered how the water was so soft that you had to take a shower afterwards to get all the soap off your body, and he remembered how the foam used to float on the surface of the water, so that you could not see your legs underneath. He remembered that sometimes they were given calcium tablets because the school doctor used to say that soft water was bad for the teeth.

'In Brighton,' he said, 'the water isn't ...'

He did not finish the sentence. Something had occurred to him; something so fantastic and absurd that for a moment he felt like telling the nurse about it and having a good laugh.

She looked up. 'The water isn't what?' she said.

'Nothing,' he answered. 'I was dreaming.'

She rinsed the flannel in the basin, wiped the soap off his leg and dried him with a towel.

'It's nice to be washed,' he said. 'I feel better.' He was feeling his face with his hand. 'I need a shave.'

'We'll do that tomorrow,' she said. 'Perhaps you can do it yourself then.'

That night he could not sleep. He lay awake thinking of the Junkers 88s and of the hardness of the water. He could think of nothing else. They were Ju-88s, he said to himself. I know they were. And yet it is not possible, because they would not be flying around so low over here in broad daylight. I know that it is true and yet I know that it is impossible. Perhaps I am ill. Perhaps I am behaving like a fool and do not know what I am doing or saying. Perhaps I am delirious. For a long time he lay awake thinking these things, and once he sat up in bed and said aloud, 'I will prove that I am not crazy. I will make a little speech about something complicated and intellectual. I will talk about what to do with Germany after the war.' But before he had time to begin, he was asleep.

He woke just as the first light of day was showing through the slit in the curtains over the window. The room was still dark, but he could tell that it was already beginning to get light outside. He lay looking at the grey light which was showing through the slit in the curtain and as he lay there he remembered the day before. He remembered the Junkers 88s and the hardness of the water; he remembered the large pleasant nurse and the kind doctor, and now a small grain of doubt took root in his mind and it began to grow.

He looked around the room. The nurse had taken the roses out the night before. There was nothing except the table with a packet of cigarettes, a box of matches and an ashtray. The room was bare. It was no longer warm or friendly. It was not even comfortable. It was cold and empty and very quiet.

Slowly the grain of doubt grew, and with it came fear, a light, dancing fear that warned but did not frighten; the kind of fear that one gets not because one is afraid, but because one feels that there is something wrong. Quickly the doubt and the fear grew so that he became restless and angry, and when he touched his forehead with his hand, he found that it was damp with sweat. He knew then that he must do something; that he must find some way of proving to himself that he was either right or wrong, and he looked up and saw again the window and the green curtains. From where he lay, that window was right in front of him, but it was fully ten yards away. Somehow he must reach it and look out. The idea became an obsession with him and soon he could think of nothing except the window. But what about his leg? He put his hand underneath the bedclothes and felt the thick bandaged stump which was all that was left on the right hand side. It seemed all right. It didn't hurt. But it would not be easy.

He sat up. Then he pushed the bedclothes aside and put his left leg on the floor. Slowly, carefully, he swung his body over until he had both hands on the floor as well; then he was out of bed, kneeling on the carpet. He looked at the stump. It was very short and thick, covered with bandages. It was beginning to hurt and he could feel it throbbing. He wanted to collapse, lie down on the carpet and do nothing, but he knew that he must go on.

With two arms and one leg, he crawled over towards the window. He would reach forward as far as he could with his arms, then he would give a little jump and slide his left leg along after them. Each time he did it, it jarred his wound so that he gave a soft grunt of pain, but he continued to crawl across the floor on two hands and one knee. When he got to the window he reached up, and one at a time he placed both hands on the sill. Slowly he raised himself up until he was standing on his left leg. Then quickly he pushed aside the curtains and looked out.

He saw a small house with a grey tiled roof standing alone beside a narrow lane, and immediately behind it there was a ploughed field. In front of the house there was an untidy garden, and there was a green hedge separating the garden from the lane. He was looking at the hedge when he saw the sign. It was just a piece of board nailed to the top of a short pole, and because the hedge had not been trimmed for a long time, the branches had grown out around the sign so that it seemed almost as though it had been placed in the middle of the hedge. There was something written on the board with white paint. He pressed his head against the glass of the window, trying to read what it said. The first letter was a G, he could see that. The second was an A, and the third was an R. One after another he managed to see what the letters were. There were three words, and slowly he spelled the letters out aloud to himself as he managed to read them. G-A-R-D-E A-U C-H-I-E-N, *Garde au chien*. That is what it said.

He stood there balancing on one leg and holding tightly to the edges of the window sill with his hands, staring at the sign and at the whitewashed lettering of the words. For a moment he could think of nothing at all. He stood there looking at the sign, repeating the words over and over to himself. Slowly he began to realize the full meaning of the thing. He looked up at the cottage and at the ploughed field. He looked at the small orchard on the left of the cottage and he looked at the green countryside beyond. 'So this is France,' he said. 'I am in France.'

Now the throbbing in his right thigh was very great. It felt as though someone was pounding the end of his stump with a hammer and suddenly the pain became so intense that it affected his head. For a moment he thought he was going to fall. Quickly he knelt down again, crawled back to the bed and hoisted himself in. He pulled the bedclothes over himself and lay back on the pillow, exhausted. He could still think of nothing at all except the small sign by the hedge and the ploughed field and the orchard. It was the words on the sign that he could not forget.

It was some time before the nurse came in. She came carrying a basin of hot water and she said, 'Good morning, how are you today?'

He said, 'Good morning, nurse.'

The pain was still great under the bandages, but he did not wish to tell this woman anything. He looked at her as she busied herself with getting the washing things ready. He looked at her more carefully now. Her hair was very fair. She was tall and big-boned and her face seemed pleasant. But there was something a little uneasy about her eyes. They were never still. They never looked at anything for more than a moment and they moved too quickly from one place to another in the room. There was something about her movements also. They were too sharp and nervous to go well with the casual manner in which she spoke.

She set down the basin, took off his pyjama top and began to wash him.

'Did you sleep well?'

'Yes.'

'Good,' she said. She was washing his arms and his chest.

'I believe there's someone coming down to see you from the Air Ministry after breakfast,' she went on. 'They want a report or something. I expect you know all about it. How you got shot down and all that. I won't let him stay long, so don't worry.'

He did not answer. She finished washing him and gave him a toothbrush and some toothpowder. He brushed his teeth, rinsed his mouth and spat the water out into the basin.

Later she brought him his breakfast on a tray, but he did not want to eat. He was still feeling weak and sick and he wished only to lie still and think about what had happened. And there was a sentence running through his head. It was a sentence which Johnny, the Intelligence Officer of his squadron, always repeated to the pilots every day before they went out. He could see Johnny now, leaning against the wall of the dispersal hut with his pipe in his hand, saying, 'And if they get you, don't forget, just your name, rank and number. Nothing else. For God's sake, say nothing else.'

'There you are,' she said as she put the tray on his lap. 'I've got you an egg. Can you manage all right?'

'Yes.'

She stood beside the bed. 'Are you feeling all right?'

'Yes.'

'Good. If you want another egg I might be able to get you one.'

'This is all right.'

'Well, just ring the bell if you want any more.' And she went out.

He had just finished eating, when the nurse came in again.

She said, 'Wing Commander Roberts is here. I've told him that he can only stay for a few minutes.'

She beckoned with her hand and the Wing Commander came in.

'Sorry to bother you like this,' he said.

He was an ordinary R.A.F. officer, dressed in a uniform which was a little shabby. He wore wings and a D.F.C. He was fairly tall and thin with plenty of black hair. His teeth, which were irregular and widely spaced, stuck out a little even when he closed his mouth. As he spoke he took a printed form and a pencil from his pocket and he pulled up a chair and sat down.

'How are you feeling?'

There was no answer.

'Tough luck about your leg. I know how you feel. I hear you put up a fine show before they got you.'

The man in the bed was lying quite still, watching the man in the chair.

The man in the chair said, 'Well, let's get this stuff over. I'm afraid you'll have to answer a few questions so that I can fill in this combat report. Let me see now, first of all, what was your squadron?'

The man in the bed did not move. He looked straight at the Wing Commander and he said, 'My name is Peter Williamson, My rank is Squadron Leader and my number is nine seven two four five seven.'

Only This

That night the frost was very heavy. It covered the hedges and whitened the grass in the fields so that it seemed almost as though it had been snowing. But the night was clear and beautiful and bright with stars, and the moon was nearly full.

The cottage stood alone in a corner of the big field. There was a path from the front door which led across the field to a stile and on over the next field to a gate which opened on to the lane about three miles from the village. There were no other houses in sight and the country around was open and flat and many of the fields were under the plough because of the war.

The light of the moon shone upon the cottage. It shone through the open window into the bedroom where the woman was asleep. She slept lying on her back, with her face upturned to the ceiling, with her long hair spread out around her on the pillow, and although she was asleep, her face was not the face of someone who is resting. Once she had been beautiful, but now there were thin furrows running across her forehead and there was a tightness about the way in which her skin was stretched over the cheekbones. But her mouth was still gentle, and as she slept, she did not close her lips.

The bedroom was small, with a low ceiling, and for furniture there was a dressing-table and an armchair. The clothes of the woman lay over the back of the armchair where she had put them when she undressed. Her black shoes were on the floor beside the chair. On the dressing-table there was a hairbrush, a letter and a large photograph of a young boy in uniform who wore a pair of wings on the left side of his tunic. It was a smiling photograph, the kind that one likes to send to one's mother and it had a thin, black frame made of wood. The

144

moon shone through the open window and the woman slept
her restless sleep. There was no noise anywhere save for the
soft, regular noise of her breathing and the rustle of the bedclothes as she stirred in her sleep.

Then, from far away, there came a deep, gentle rumble
which grew and grew and became louder and louder until soon
the whole sky seemed to be filled with a great noise which
throbbed and throbbed and kept on throbbing and did not stop.

Right at the beginning, even before it came close, the woman
had heard the noise. In her sleep she had been waiting for it,
listening for the noise and dreading the moment when it would
come. When she heard it, she opened her eyes and for a while
she lay quite still, listening. Then she sat up, pushed the bedclothes aside and got out of bed. She went over to the window
and placing her hands on the window sill, she leaned out,
looking up into the sky; and her long hair fell down over her
shoulders, over the thin cotton nightdress which she wore. For
many minutes she stood there in the cold, leaning out of the
window, hearing the noise, looking up and searching the sky;
but she saw only the bright moon and the stars.

'God keep you,' she said aloud. 'Oh dear God keep you
safe.'

Then she turned and went quickly over to the bed, pulled the
blankets away and wrapped them round her shoulders like a
shawl. She slipped her bare feet into the black shoes and
walked over to the armchair and pushed it forward so that it
was right up in front of the window. Then she sat down.

The noise and the throbbing overhead was very great. For a
long time it continued as the huge procession of bombers
moved towards the south. All the while the woman sat
huddled in her blankets, looking out of the window into the
sky.

Then it was over. Once more the night became silent. The
frost lay heavy on the field and on the hedges and it seemed as
though the whole countryside was holding its breath. An army
was marching in the sky. All along the route people had heard
the noise and knew what it was; they knew that soon, even
before they had gone to sleep, there would be a battle. Men

drinking beer in the pubs had stopped their talking in order to listen. Families in their houses had turned off the radio and gone out into their gardens, where they stood looking up into the sky. Soldiers arguing in their tents had stopped their shouting, and men and women walking home at night from the factories had stood still on the road, listening to the noise.

It is always the same. As the bombers move south across the country at night, the people who hear them become strangely silent. For those women whose men are with the planes, the moment is not an easy one to bear.

Now they had gone, and the woman lay back in the armchair and closed her eyes, but she did not sleep. Her face was white and the skin seemed to have been drawn tightly over her cheeks and gathered up in wrinkles around her eyes. Her lips were parted and it was as though she were listening to someone talking. Almost she could hear the sound of his voice as he used to call to her from outside the window when he came back from working in the fields. She could hear him saying he was hungry and asking what there was for supper, and then when he came in he would put his arm around her shoulder and talk to her about what he had been doing all day. She would bring in the supper and he would sit down and start to eat and always he would say, why don't you have some and she never knew what to answer except that she wasn't hungry. She would sit and watch him and pour out his tea, and after a while she would take his plate and go out into the kitchen to get him some more.

It was not easy having only one child. The emptiness when he was not there and the knowing all the time that something might happen; the deep conscious knowing that there was nothing else to live for except this; that if something did happen, then you too would be dead. There would be no use in sweeping the floor or washing the dishes or cleaning the house; there would be no use in gathering wood for the fire or in feeding the hens; there would be no use in living.

Now, as she sat there by the open window she did not feel the cold; she felt only a great loneliness and a great fear. The fear took hold of her and grew upon her so that she could not bear it, and she got up from the chair and leaned out of the window again, looking up into the sky. And as she looked the night was no longer beautiful; it was cold and clear and immensely dangerous. She did not see the fields or the hedges or the carpet of frost upon the countryside; she saw only the depths of the sky and the danger that was there.

Slowly she turned and sank down again into her chair. Now the fear was great. She could think of nothing at all except that she must see him and be with him, that she must see him now because tomorrow would be too late. She let her head rest against the back of the chair and when she closed her eyes she saw the aircraft; she saw it clearly in the moonlight, moving forward through the night like a great, black bird. She was close to it and she could see the way in which the nose of the machine reached out far ahead of everything, as though the bird was craning its neck in the eagerness of its passage. She could see the markings on the wings and on the body and she knew that he was inside. Twice she called to him, but there was no answer; then the fear and the longing welled up within her so that she could stand it no longer and it carried her forward through the night and on and on until she was with him, beside him, so close that she could have touched him had she put out her hand.

He was sitting at the controls with gloves on his hands, dressed in a great bulky flying-suit which made his body look huge and shapeless and twice its normal size. He was looking straight ahead at the instruments on the panel, concentrating upon what he was doing and thinking of nothing except flying the machine.

Now she called to him again and he heard her. He looked around and when he saw her, he smiled and stretched out a hand and touched her shoulder, and then all the fear and the loneliness and the longing went out of her and she was happy.

For a long time she stood beside him watching him as he flew the machine. Every now and then he would look around and smile at her, and once he said something, but she could not hear what it was because of the noise of the engines. Suddenly he pointed ahead through the glass windshield of the aeroplane and she saw that the sky was full of searchlights. There were many hundreds of them; long white fingers of light travelling lazily across the sky, swaying this way and that, working in unison so that sometimes several of them would come together and meet in the same spot and after a while they would separate and meet again somewhere else, all the time searching the night for the bombers which were moving in on the target.

Behind the searchlights she saw the flak. It was coming up from the town in a thick many-coloured curtain, and the flash of the shells as they burst in the sky lit up the inside of the bomber.

He was looking straight ahead now, concentrating upon the flying, weaving through the searchlights and going directly into this curtain of flak, and she watched and waited and did not dare to move or to speak lest she distract him from his task.

She knew that they had been hit when she saw the flames from the nearest engine on the left side. She watched them through the glass of the side panel, licking against the surface of the wing as the wind blew them backwards, and she watched them take hold of the wing and come dancing over the black surface until they were right up under the cockpit itself. At first she was not frightened. She could see him sitting there, very cool, glancing continually to one side, watching the flames and flying the machine, and once he looked quickly around and smiled at her and she knew then that there was no danger. All around she saw the searchlights and the flak and the explosions of the flak and the colours of the tracer, and the sky was not a sky but just a small confined space which was so full of lights and explosions that it did not seem possible that one could fly through it.

But the flames were brighter now on the left wing. They had spread over the whole surface. They were alive and active, feeding on the fabric, leaning backwards in the wind which fanned them and encouraged them and gave them no chance of going out.

Then came the explosion. There was a blinding white flash and a hollow *crumph* as though someone had burst a blown-up paper bag; then there was nothing but flames and thick whitish-grey smoke. The flames were coming up through the floor and through the sides of the cockpit; the smoke was so thick that it was difficult to see and almost impossible to breathe. She became terrified and panicky because he was still sitting there at the controls, flying the machine, fighting to keep it on an even keel, turning the wheel first to one side, then to the other, and suddenly there was a blast of cold air and she had a vague impression of urgent crouching figures scrambling past her and throwing themselves away from the burning aircraft.

Now the whole thing was a mass of flames and through the smoke she could see him still sitting there, fighting with the wheel while the crew got out, and as he did so he held one arm up over his face because the heat was so great. She rushed forward and took him by the shoulders and shook him and shouted, 'Come on, quickly, you must get out, quickly, quickly.'

Then she saw that his head had fallen forward upon his chest and that he was limp and unconscious. Frantically she tried to pull him out of the seat and towards the door, but he was too limp and heavy. The smoke was filling her lungs and her throat so that she began to retch and gasp for breath. She was hysterical now, fighting against death and against everything and she managed to get her hands under his arms and drag him a little way towards the door. But it was impossible to get him farther. His legs were tangled around the wheel and there was a buckle somewhere which she could not undo. She knew then that it was impossible, that there was no hope because of the smoke and the fire and because there was no time; and suddenly all the strength drained out of her body. She fell down on top of him and began to cry as she had never cried before.

Then came the spin and the fierce rushing dive downwards and she was thrown forward into the fire so that the last she knew was the bright yellow of the flames and the smell of the burning.

Her eyes were closed and her head was resting against the back of the chair. Her hands were clutching the edges of the blankets as though she were trying to pull them tighter around her body and her long hair fell down over her shoulders.

Outside the moon was low in the sky. The frost lay heavier than ever on the fields and on the hedges and there was no noise anywhere. Then from far away in the south came a deep gentle rumble which grew and grew and became louder and louder until soon the whole sky was filled with the noise and the singing of those who were coming back.

But the woman who sat by the window never moved. She had been dead for some time.

Someone Like You

'Beer?'

'Yes, beer.'

I gave the order and the waiter brought the bottles and two glasses. We poured out our own, tipping the glasses and holding the tops of the bottles close to the glass.

'Cheers,' I said.

He nodded. We lifted our glasses and drank.

It was five years since I had seen him, and during that time he had been fighting the war. He had been fighting it right from the beginning up to now and I saw at once how he had changed. From being a young, bouncing boy, he had become someone old and wise and gentle. He had become gentle like a wounded child. He had become old like a tired man of seventy years. He had become so different and he had changed so much that at first it was embarrassing for both of us and it was not easy to know what to say.

He had been flying in France in the early days and he was in Britain during the Battle. He was in the Western Desert when we had nothing and he was in Greece and Crete. He was in Syria and he was at Habbaniya during the rebellion. He was at Alamein. He had been flying in Sicily and in Italy and then he had gone back and flown again from England. Now he was an old man.

He was small, not more than five feet six, and he had a pale, wide-open face which did not hide anything, and a sharp pointed chin. His eyes were bright and dark. They were never still unless they were looking into your own. His hair was black and untidy. There was a wisp of it always hanging down over his forehead; he kept pushing it back with his hand.

For a while we were awkward and did not speak. He was sitting opposite me at the table, leaning forward a little, drawing lines on the dew of the cold beer-glass with his finger. He was looking at the glass, pretending to concentrate upon what he was doing, and to me it seemed as though he had something to say, but that he did not know how to say it. I sat there and picked nuts out of the plate and munched them noisily, pretending that I did not care about anything, not even about making a noise while eating.

Then without stopping his drawing on the glass and without looking up, he said quietly and very slowly, 'Oh God, I wish I was a waiter or a whore or something.'

He picked up his glass and drank the beer slowly and all at once, in two swallows. I knew now that there was something on his mind and I knew that he was gathering courage so that he could speak.

'Let's have another,' I said.

'Yes, let's have a whisky.'

'All right, whisky.'

I ordered two double Scotches and some soda, and we poured the soda into the Scotch and drank. He picked up his glass and drank, put it down, picked it up again and drank some more. As he put down the glass the second time, he leaned forward and quite suddenly he began to talk.

'You know,' he said, 'you know I keep thinking during a raid, when we are running over the target, just as we are going to release our bombs, I keep thinking to myself, shall I just jink a little; shall I swerve a fraction to one side, then my bombs will fall on someone else. I keep thinking, whom shall I make them fall on; whom shall I kill tonight. Which ten, twenty or a hundred people shall I kill tonight. It is all up to me. And now I think about this every time I go out.'

He had taken a small nut and was splitting it into pieces with his thumb-nail as he spoke, looking down at what he was doing because he was embarrassed by his own talk.

He was speaking very slowly. 'It would just be a gentle pressure with the ball of my foot upon the rudder-bar; a pressure so slight that I would hardly know that I was doing it,

152

and it would throw the bombs on to a different house and on to other people. It is all up to me, the whole thing is up to me, and each time that I go out I have to decide which ones shall be killed. I can do it with the gentle pressure of the ball of my foot upon the rudder-bar. I can do it so that I don't even notice that it is being done. I just lean a little to one side because I am shifting my sitting position. That is all I am doing, and then I kill a different lot of people.'

Now there was no dew left upon the face of the glass, but he was still running the fingers of his right hand up and down the smooth surface.

'Yes,' he said, 'it is a complicated thought. It is very far-reaching; and when I am bombing I cannot get it out of my mind. You see it is such a gentle pressure with the ball of the foot; just a touch on the rudder-bar and the bomb-aimer wouldn't even notice. Each time I go out, I say to myself, shall it be these or shall it be those? Which ones are the worst? Perhaps if I make a little skid to the left I will get a houseful of lousy women-shooting German soldiers, or perhaps if I make that little skid I will miss getting the soldiers and get an old man in a shelter. How can I know? How can anyone know these things?'

He paused and pushed his empty glass away from him into the middle of the table.

'And so I never jink,' he added, 'at least hardly ever.'

'I jinked once,' I said, 'ground-strafing. I thought I'd kill the ones on the other side of the road instead.'

'Everybody jinks,' he said. 'Shall we have another drink?'

'Yes, let's have another.'

I called the waiter and gave the order, and while we were waiting, we sat looking around the room at the other people. The place was starting to fill up because it was about six o'clock and we sat there looking at the people who were coming in. They were standing around looking for tables, sitting down, laughing and ordering drinks.

'Look at that woman,' I said. 'The one just sitting down over there.'

'What about her?'

'Wonderful figure,' I said. 'Wonderful bosom. Look at her bosom.'

The waiter brought the drinks.

'Did I ever tell you about Stinker?' he said.

'Stinker who?'

'Stinker Sullivan in Malta.'

'No.'

'About Stinker's dog?'

'No.'

'Stinker had a dog, a great big Alsatian, and he loved that dog as though it was his father and his mother and everything else he had, and the dog loved Stinker. It used to follow him around everywhere he went, and when he went on ops it used to sit on the tarmac outside the hangars waiting for him to come back. It was called Smith. Stinker really loved that dog. He loved it like his mother and he used to talk to it all day long.'

'Lousy whisky,' I said.

'Yes, let's have another.'

We got some more whisky.

'Well anyway,' he went on, 'one day the squadron got orders to fly to Egypt. We had to go at once; not in two hours or later in the day, but at once. And Stinker couldn't find his dog. Couldn't find Smith anywhere. Started running all over the aerodrome yelling for Smith and going mad yelling at everyone asking where he was and yelling Smith Smith all over the aerodrome. Smith wasn't anywhere.'

'Where was he?' I said.

'He wasn't there and we had to go. Stinker had to go without Smith and he was mad as a hatter. His crew said he kept calling up over the radio asking if they'd found him. All the way to Heliopolis he kept calling up Malta saying, have you got Smith, and Malta kept saying no, they hadn't.'

'This whisky is really terrible,' I said.

'Yes. We must have some more.'

We had a waiter who was very quick.

'I was telling you about Stinker,' he said.

'Yes, tell me about Stinker.'

'Well, when we got to Egypt he wouldn't talk about anything except Smith. He used to walk around acting as though the dog was always with him. Damn fool walked around saying, "Come on, Smith, old boy, come on," and he kept looking down and talking to him as he walked along. Kept reaching down and patting the air and stroking this bloody dog that wasn't there.'

'Where was it?'

'Malta, I suppose. Must have been in Malta.'

'Isn't this awful whisky?'

'Terrible. We must have some more when we've finished this.'

'Cheers.'

'Cheers.'

'Waiter. Oh waiter. Yes; again.'

'So Smith was in Malta.'

'Yes,' he said. 'And this damn fool Stinker Sullivan went on like this right up to the time he was killed.'

'Must have been mad.'

'He was. Mad as a hatter. You know once he walked into the Sporting Club at Alexandria at drinking time.'

'That wasn't so mad.'

'He walked into the big lounge and as he went in he held the door open and started calling his dog. Then when he thought the dog had come in, he closed the door and started walking right down the length of the room, stopping every now and then and looking round and saying, "Come on, Smith, old boy, come on." He kept flipping his fingers. Once he got down under a table where two men and two women were drinking. He got on to his hands and knees and said, "Smith, come on out of there; come here at once," and he put out his hand and started dragging nothing at all from under the table. Then he apologized to the people at the table. "This is the hell of a dog," he said to them. You should have seen their faces. He went on like that all down the room and when he came to the other end he held the door open for the dog to go out and then went out after it.'

'Man was mad.'

'Mad as a hatter. And you should have seen their faces. It was full of people drinking and they didn't know whether it was them who were crazy or whether it was Stinker. They kept looking up at each other to make sure that they weren't the only ones who couldn't see the dog. One man dropped his drink.'

'That was awful.'

'Terrible.'

The waiter came and went. The room was full of people now, all sitting at little tables, talking and drinking and wearing their uniforms. The pilot poked the ice down into his glass with his finger.

'He used to jink too,' he said.

'Who?'

'Stinker. He used to talk about it.'

'Jinking isn't anything,' I said. 'It's like not touching the cracks on the pavement when you're walking along.'

'Balls. That's just personal. Doesn't affect anyone else.'

'Well, it's like car-waiting.'

'What's car-waiting?'

'I always do it,' I said.

'What is it?'

'Just as you're going to drive off, you sit back and count twenty, then you drive off.'

'You're mad too,' he said. 'You're like Stinker.'

'It's a wonderful way to avoid accidents. I've never had one in a car yet; at least, not a bad one.'

'You're drunk.'

'No, I always do it.'

'Why?'

'Because then if someone was going to have stepped off the kerb in front of your car, you won't hit them because you started later. You were delayed because you counted twenty, and the person who stepped off the kerb whom you would have hit – you missed him.'

'Why?'

'He stepped off the kerb long before you got there because you counted twenty.'

'That's a good idea.'

'I know it's a good idea.'

'It's a bloody marvellous idea.'

'I've saved lots of lives. And you can drive straight across intersections because the car you would have hit has already gone by. It went by just a little earlier because you delayed yourself by counting twenty.'

'Marvellous.'

'Isn't it?'

'But it's like jinking,' he said. 'You never really know what would have happened.'

'I always do it,' I said.

We kept right on drinking.

'Look at that woman,' I said.

'The one with the bosom?'

'Yes, marvellous bosom.'

He said slowly, 'I bet I've killed lots of women more beautiful than that one.'

'Not lots with bosoms like that.'

'I'll bet I have. Shall we have another drink?'

'Yes, one for the road.'

'There aren't any other women with bosoms like that,' I said. 'Not in Germany anyway.'

'Oh yes there are. I've killed lots of them.'

'All right. You've killed lots of women with wonderful bosoms.'

He leaned back and waved his hand around the room. 'See all the people in this room,' he said.

'Yes.'

'Wouldn't there be a bloody row if they were all suddenly dead; if they all suddenly fell off their chairs on to the floor dead?'

'What about it?'

'Wouldn't there be a bloody row?'

'Certainly there'd be a row.'

'If all the waiters got together and put stuff in all the drinks and everyone died.'

'There'd be a godalmighty row.'

'Well, I've done that hundreds of times. I've killed more

people than there are in this room hundreds of times. So have
you.'

'Lots more,' I said. 'But that's different.'

'Same sort of people. Men and women and waiters. All
drinking in a pub.'

'That's different.'

'Like hell it is. Wouldn't there be a bloody row if it happened
here?'

'Bloody awful row.'

'But we've done it. Lots of times.'

'Hundreds of times,' I said. 'This is nothing.'

'This is a lousy place.'

'Yes, it's lousy. Let's go somewhere else.'

'Finish our drinks.'

We finished our drinks and we both tried to pay the bill, so
we tossed for it and I won. It came to sixteen dollars and
twenty-five cents. He gave the waiter a two-dollar tip.

We got up and walked around the tables and over to the
door.

'Taxi,' he said.

'Yes, must have a taxi.'

There wasn't a doorman. We stood out on the kerb waiting
for a taxi to come along and he said, 'This is a good town.'

'Wonderful town,' I said. I felt fine. It was dark outside, but
there were a few street-lamps, and we could see the cars going
by and the people walking on the other side of the street. There
was a thin, quiet drizzle falling, and the wetness on the black
street shone yellow under the lights of the cars and under the
street-lamps. The tyres of the cars hissed on the wet surface.

'Let's go to a place which has lots of whisky,' he said. 'Lots
of whisky and a man with egg on his beard serving it.'

'Fine.'

'Somewhere where there are no other people but just us and
the man with egg on his beard. Either that.'

'Yes,' I said. 'Either that or what?'

'Or a place with a hundred thousand people in it.'

'Yes,' I said. 'O.K.'

We stood there waiting and we could see the lights of the

cars as they came round the bend over to the left, coming towards us with the tyres swishing on the wet surface and going past us up the road to the bridge which goes over the river. We could see the drizzle falling through the beams of their headlights and we stood there waiting for a taxi.